SYNOPSIS

Kennedy:

Once I was released from prison, I thought that all of the heartache was over. I was back with my family, and I assumed that the nightmare had come to an end. Little did I know, the nightmare had actually just begun. Everybody around me was keeping secrets that would send me right back to a dark place; a place way worse than the prison that I had just emerged from. This time of my life was supposed to be my "happily ever after the bullshit." King's empire was bringing in more money than he could count. I was about to get the wedding of my dreams. On the outside, things looked so perfect, and I was beyond happy. In fact, I was so happy that I didn't see the deceit that was happening right under my nose.

They say that every friendship, every relationship, is bound to fall apart when you start keeping secrets. That couldn't be truer with King, Meech, Siren, Dolla and Jada. They were all keeping secrets that would tear apart our family and our business, and I was too busy in my own immense happiness to even see it.

But soon I would.

Merely weeks after my release, I would find myself, once again, in a world that was turned upside down, and yet again, all of the blame would fall on my undying loyalty to my King.

DAVID WEAVER PRESENTS

A Thug's LOVE 2

JESSICA N. WATKINS

PREVIOUSLY ON A THUG'S LOVE

SIREN

Meech had kicked me out of the house with nothing. I didn't have a cell phone, a purse, or even a wallet. All I was wearing were the leggings, sports bra and flip-flops that I had been lounging around the house in. I was walking down the main street near our community. I was on my way to the lounge that Meech and I frequented. I was cool with the bartenders and owners, so I figured that I could use one of their phones to call my mom or get a ride to the city.

"Siren!"

My eyes rolled into the back of my head as soon as I heard her irritating, Latin accent.

"Not now!" I screeched over my shoulder. "I don't feel like your shit today!"

I could hear the engine of her car turning off.

"Urgh. Now I gotta deal with this bitch," I muttered under my breath as I slowed my pace. I hated to even be bothered with her, but at the moment I needed a friend, and after all these years, Detective Sanchez had become a friend. It was easy for two people from two different paths to become friends when they had the same enemy.

Plus, I figured she could give me a ride.

I could hear the heels of her shoes against the pavement, so I turned around reluctantly. I wasn't worried about Meech seeing me because he looked like he never wanted to see my ass again, so him coming to look for me was out of the fucking question.

"What's up, Maria?" At this point, me and Detective Sanchez were on a first name basis.

She walked toward me with a half-smile. "What are you doing walking out here? And why aren't you answering your phone?"

"I don't have my fucking phone." Then I sighed, revealing, "Meech kicked me out."

She chuckled. "Damn."

"Fuck you, Maria. This isn't funny." We had a bit of a love-hate relationship. "What do you want?"

"Pieces of Lock's body have been found in an alley in the city. I know he's done some work for King's crew in the past. You hear anything about a murder? Maybe they thought Lock was the snitch that was leading us to them regarding Terry's murder?"

I shrugged my shoulders with irritation. "I don't know, Maria."

Her head cocked to the side, causing her authentic red curls to fall in her eyes. "You sure about that?"

"Hell yeah, I'm sure!" I snapped, smacking my lips.

"C'mon, Siren. I know you have more than that."

"I don't! Look, I have given you all that I can. What else do you want me to do?"

I had. After being the cause of Kennedy's arrest, I felt guilty as fuck, but that only lasted for a few months. Over time, the guilt subsided and my love–hate relationship with King once again took over. I wanted that nigga gone, but I wanted him with me at the same time. So after Kennedy was gone for a while, I tried my luck.

A year after Kennedy had been locked up, King was still just a shell of the person he'd once been. He had lost weight, was unusually quiet, and had stayed to himself. All he could think about was his hustle and Kayla. I'd figured that he was dying for the love and affection of someone familiar, and although I was his best friend's woman, I'd figured that he would remember the nights that I had taken care of him and his needs. But once again, he shut me down cold, looking at me like I was so unworthy of being with the *infamous King*.

His rejection had only fueled my obsession. I was angry that he hadn't seen in me what he had seen in so many other bitches. Every time I wondered what was better about a bitch in prison than me standing in front of him with an eager, wet, and ready mouth and pussy, my anger grew. Who the fuck did he think he was? A king, that's what! That nigga really thought he was fucking royalty, and apparently, I was a peasant. Then when Kennedy got out and he acted like the fucking queen of England was arriving in the Chi, my love turned to pure hate once again.

I'd called Maria and told her about the night Meech had come home drunk and talking loudly on the phone. It was the day before Kennedy's return. I was lying on the couch, pretending to be asleep, as I waited for him to come home from handling some business with Dolla. He was in the kitchen when I heard him say, "We might have to handle that nigga like we did Terry, in broad daylight in front of his family. Then he'll know not to fuck with us."

Everybody in the hood had figured that someone in King's crew was responsible for Terry's murder in retaliation for setting up Rozay. But of course, no one cared or snitched because they'd figured Terry had deserved it for even attempting to come against the infamous King and his crew. But I was more than ready to come against him as I watched King literally praise Kennedy's ass as he prepared for her homecoming. The sacrifice that she had made had gained her so much undying loyalty from him. The nigga hadn't even touched a piece of pussy in the time she was gone. She had made one fucking heroic move, and she was a saint in his eyes. But everything that I'd done had gone overlooked.

So the morning of Kennedy's return, I'd called Maria and told her about what I'd heard Meech say, and gave her information about the van I'd seen them all climb into a few hours before Terry's murder. I knew that the information would most likely lead to Dolla and Meech's arrest as well, and the demise of their entire empire. But I didn't give a fuck, as long as King would be rotting in jail.

It just wasn't fair! He was so happy, walking around like he didn't have a care in the world, especially not for me, when my heart ached every time my son asked for his father.

I just wanted him to hurt like I had been for years.

"Just go arrest his ass," I spat with a frown. Just thinking of him irritated my soul. Everything was his fault. My constant unhappiness was his fault because nothing made me happy because I wasn't with him—not even Meech. At that moment, as I stood now without a home, it was all King's fault because my dumb ass was protecting him while I lied to everyone about who Elijah's father was.

"I want to!" Maria responded. "That slick motherfucker is airtight. None of my evidence against him will hold up in court."

"Well, what the fuck else do you want me to do?"

"Testify against him."

"Are you crazy?" I asked with a possessed chuckle.

Maria came toward me with a look of desperation. "Your testimony will put him away for good."

I hated King, but I liked living. "I can't, Maria."

"Then I'll use what I have to arrest Meech," she threatened.

That was always her stronghold over me. She always threatened me with arresting Meech every time her bipolar ass came around with a new obsession over locking King up. But as the years went by, there was rarely anything that I could give her. I was Meech's woman, so my involvement in the business became less and less. He rarely told me anything, and telling her about any drops that me and Jada did weren't an option because I wasn't about to send me or her to jail. I'd had nothing until I overheard Meech's drunk ass talking about Terry's murder.

"That ain't gon' work this time," I muttered as I waved my hand dismissively. "That nigga don't want me no more. He just literally put me out on the street. Do what you gotta do."

Maria looked at me like she was disappointed with my defeated spirit. "Come on, Siren. I'll give you a ride. Where are you..."

My attention went away from Maria as I looked up the street.

"Get out of here!" I spat as I noticed Jada's Range Rover coming our way.

Maria looked at me like I was crazy as I began to speed walk away from her. "What's–"

"Go!" I spat over my shoulder. "Just go!"

Then I heard Jada's familiar voice. "Siren! Siren, come here!"

JADA

Nah, don't walk away now, bitch.

I had been parked on the corner watching Siren talk to this detective for ten damn minutes! *What the fuck was she doing talking to a detective?* I thought as I watched them talk like they were the best of friends. It was apparent that they knew each other, and knew each other well.

Meech had called and asked me to come find Siren. He'd told me that they had gotten into it, and he'd kicked her out with nothing. But he wouldn't tell me what they'd gotten into it about when I'd asked. Of course, I got right up, threw some clothes on, and went looking for my girl. Imagine my surprise when I peeped her in a deep conversation with the police. She was in plain clothes, but I knew a detective when I saw one.

As soon as I started to pull up, Siren peeped me and nearly ran away from the bitch. Finally, when I began to call her name, the female detective walked away, hopped in her unmarked car, and sped off.

I called her name again. "Siren!" Finally, the heifer turned around like she had just heard me.

She looked at me and sighed with relief. "Jada, thank God! I'm so happy to see you, girl." She actually rushed toward my truck and opened the door, ignoring the confused snarl on my face. "What are you doing on this side of town?"

"Meech called me and told me to come looking for you."

A look of relief came over her. "For real? What did he say?"

"He said that y'all got into it–"

"Did he tell you why?" she asked, cutting me off with a frightened look.

"Naaah..." I spoke slowly because all of this was really throwing me off. She was acting like I hadn't just seen her talking to a detective. Plus, she was obviously scared as fuck that Meech had told me what their argument had been about. "He just wanted me to come give you a ride."

"Oh." Then both relief and disappointment filled her eyes.

I slowly pulled off as anger started boiling inside of me. This had been my best friend, my bitch, for years. I knew her. There was no fucking way she knew the police. She didn't have any friends in the department, and nobody that lived the life we lived should have been talking to the police.

Siren looked at me curiously as I pulled my truck into the alley and then parked in the back of an apartment building. "Where are we going?"

I ignored her questioning glare and killed the engine. "What the fuck were you doing hollering at the police, Siren?"

At first, she tried to play dumb. "Huh? What?"

"Don't play with me, Siren!" She was shocked, and so was I when tears came to my eyes. I was asking her, but the answer was obvious to me. There was no reason for her to be cool with a detective without me knowing unless she was on some snake shit. "I know you, bitch. I know your life. You haven't told me about having no friends in the department, but I watched you holding a conversation with that bitch. So who the fuck is she?"

Siren stared blankly out of the window as tears filled her eyes. "I don't know her. Now would you c'mon? Drive! Shit!"

I bit my lip so hard that I could damn near taste blood. "Siren, don't fucking play with me."

"I'm not!"

"You gon' sit here and lie to me?"

"I'm not–"

"Fuck that shit, Siren! Tell me the truth!"

Siren knew about Terry's murder. Although I didn't tell that to Dolla the other day, I knew that Siren had overheard Meech talking about the murder. She'd secretly told me as we got massages the day that Kennedy had gotten out. But even when Dolla told me that he had been questioned, I never even considered that it was Siren. Not my girl, not my best friend, not my *family*.

She looked at me like I was the one who was crazy. "Ain't shit to tell!" she shrieked.

I glared back at her, never backing down. "So you ain't the one that snitched?"

Before she even knew what she was doing, she looked at me with bulging eyes, as if she was wondering how I knew, but she quickly fixed her face. "What the fuck are you talking about?"

Apparently, Meech hadn't been as honest with her about what was going on as Dolla had been with me. But still, I knew it was her. After seeing her talk to that bitch cop, it all made sense.

My heart broke, and tears filled my eyes once again. "It *was* you, wasn't it?"

Siren sucked her teeth and waved her hand. "I don't know what the fuck you talkin' about."

"Really, Siren? You just gon' sit there and play stupid? How could you? Kennedy just got out and—"

"Fuck Kennedy! Fuck King!" She had become so possessed with anger that she didn't even realize it. She looked disgusted as she ranted and raved. "Fuck them, damn! Who gives a fuck?"

I sat back, looking at her with disgust. "Apparently, *you* do."

Siren finally looked me in the eyes and saw that I was reading her like a book. She thought she had been slick all of these years, but I could see that she was crushing on King, and I could see her jealously when he got with Tiana and then Kennedy. And jealousy will make you do some foul shit. "You're a fucking snitch," I said as I shook my head. "I can't believe this shit."

"You know what? Fuck this!" she snapped as she grabbed the door handle. "I ain't gotta listen to this bullshit! I'll walk!"

As she climbed out of the car, so did I. I jumped out and was about to catch up to her just as she made it to the alley. But she wasn't able to take another step before I snatched my piece from my waist, aimed at her back and pulled the trigger. The popping sound piercing the air made her jump, but she soon hit the ground. Before she could even figure out what was happening, I was standing over her. I closed my eyes with regret before aiming at her head and pulling the trigger. I couldn't even watch as I killed my best friend, but as I turned and ran away from her bleeding and dying body, I knew it was what had to be done. I loved her like a sister, but she had come against others that I loved, and nobody came against my family.

****

I cried the entire way home. It hurt my heart that Siren was gone and that I would never hear her laugh again. I would never be able to gossip with her again, but I felt no guilt that I was the one who had taken her away from me.

"Baby? What's wrong?"

I had come into the house with tears streaming down my face. Dolla dropped the Xbox controller and immediately ran toward me as I closed the door. I fell into his arms and sobbed aloud as I held him tightly.

"Bae, please talk to me," he begged as he kissed the top of my head. "What's wrong?"

"It was *Siren*!" I cried.

"What? What was Siren?"

I breathed in deeply and attempted to stop my tears. I knew that I had to get it together in order to tell Dolla everything. And I did. I let him go, wiped my face, and walked toward the couch with him on my heels. I was still shaking as he sat closely beside me and held my hand.

"When I went looking for Siren, I found her standing on the street talking to a detective. She was in plain clothes, but I peeped the unmarked car. She was a Latino, redhead, just like the bitch that you said pulled you over the other day."

13

Tears still silently slid down my face as I recalled the moments that I knew I would never forget. "I pulled over at the corner and watched her have this deep-ass discussion with the chick. When I couldn't take it anymore, I pulled off and drove toward her. When she saw me, she hit it one way, and the detective hit it in another. I knew something was up. Siren got in my car like nothing had even happened." I shook my head, still disappointed in her. "I asked her what she was doing talking to a cop, and she played dumb. It was obvious right then! Baby, she knew about Terry's murder—"

"No, she didn't. Meech said he—"

"Meech never told her, but she overheard him talking about it a few days ago."

His eyes bucked. "Why didn't you tell me?!"

"I told Siren I wouldn't! I'm sorry!" I cried.

Dolla shook his head in disbelief. "Why would she snitch? Bae, I don't think Siren would do that."

"She had to. She overheard Meech talking, and then the police showed up the next day questioning you? That shit ain't no coincidence! We were there that day when y'all left. We saw y'all in the van, remember?"

It took Dolla a few minutes to take it all in, but when he did and realized the truth, his face fell in his hands as his head shook with regret.

"That bitch has been lying to me! To *me*, her best fucking friend. And then she snitched on my niggas! On Meech and King! On my family! How could she?" I shook my head, the heartbreak causing a pain I had never felt before.

"Why the fuck would she snitch?"

I sucked my teeth. "She kept acting like I didn't know what I was talking about, but that bitch was lying! I could tell."

Dolla looked into the air with disappointment. It had finally all made sense to him too. Siren was a snitch. "So what's gon' stop her from telling some other shit?"

Tears filled my eyes again as I admitted, "She's not going to say anything else because I...killed her."

I didn't even see Dolla's reaction because I threw my face into my hands and began to sob. I could feel his arms wrapped tightly around me as his phone rang. He continued holding me as he answered. "What up, Meech?"

I instantly sat up and shot bulging eyes at Dolla as I heard Meech ask, "Aye, bruh, did Jada get back? She ain't answerin' her phone."

"Yeah, she's back. She's in the shower."

"Did she find Siren?"

"Nah, man. I was just about to call you. She said she didn't see her."

"Oh...a'ight then."

"Call her mama's house. Maybe she got a ride there."

"Nah, it's all good. I don't care that much. Fuck that bitch."

"Damn, bruh. It's like that? What happened?"

I could tell that Dolla and I were thinking the same thing. Did they get into it because Meech had also found out that Siren was a snitch?

But he only answered, "Some bullshit, bruh. I just can't trust her ass."

"That's fucked up."

"Ain't it?" he sighed. "Well, I'll holla at you tomorrow."

"A'ight, bruh. One."

As Dolla hung up, there was an eerie feeling in the air.

"You think he found out what she did?" I asked Dolla.

"Nah, he would have told me."

"What if the police have evidence, Dolla?" I started to freak. "What if they pin this shit on y'all?"

"Nah, it's all good. Whatever she told them wasn't shit. If it was, they would have arrested us. I'm sure they were trying to get some more evidence out of her but...you took care of that."

Once again, I began to sob into my hands. I was hurt that my friend, my *best* friend, had turned against us. I was confused because I'd had no idea why. I wanted to die because now she was gone, and it was because of me.

But Dolla wrapped his arms around me and held me again, assuring me, "You did what you had to do, baby. You protected your family. And I'll protect you *forever*. No one will ever know."

KENNEDY

♪Can we stay home tonight?
Try something new tonight?
This drink got me feelin' right
I'm 'bout to lose my mind
U, Me, & Hennessy, look what you did to me
Fuckin' so crazy, you twirlin' and spinnin' me
My head keep on spinnin', my legs keep on shakin'
But my head keep on spinnin'
I'm out of my mind let's keep on sippin'
Let's make some babies, and make it official♪

King was in such a good mood that he stayed at home with Kayla and me all day, which I enjoyed. Whatever *business* that had been taking him away from home, when I had imagined spending days after my release in his arms and never coming up for air, had finally been *handled*, so he'd said. So that day, I finally got what I had been waiting for: *him*. After returning from my father's house, we watched movies, laughed, reminisced, and fantasized about Cabo while Kayla ran rampant and didn't listen to a gawd damn thing I said.

Now, King and I were soaking in the Jacuzzi in our master bathroom. Finally, after a day of acting a whole damn fool, Kayla was asleep. King had awarded my Kayla survival with Remy 1738 and his hands massaging my shoulders as I lay against his chest, sipping and listening to the surround sound while the stars winked at me through the picture window.

"Sooo..." I smiled as I waited for King to continue. I knew there was something to look forward to after that pause. "I have a surprise for you."

"What now, King?" Don't get me wrong. Surprises are always fun, but King had been suffocating me with gifts since my release. It had only been five days since I'd gotten home, and yet I had more clothes, shoes, jewelry, and trinkets than any woman could ask for.

"I'm throwing you a party for your birthday."

My face scrunched as I sipped from my glass. "But I just had a party. People are going to get tired of partying with me."

"But–"

I interrupted, "I just want to spend my birthday with you and Kayla before we leave for Cabo the next day. That's all I want."

"But it's an important party."

I sat up in the tub and turned toward him. That sneaky-ass grin on his face said that he was up to a bunch of something.

"What kind of important party, King?"

He licked his lips as he smiled. I swear I wanted to suck his dick right then. I just wanted to dive under that water and put his dick in my mouth!

He reached for me and brought me toward him. The water splashed and spilled onto the floor as we adjusted against one another. "It's our wedding."

"What?" I whispered my shock. I was surprised, but not so much that I wanted to wake up Kayla's crazy ass!

He chuckled with his answer, "I said it's *our wedding*. That's your birthday party."

"Oh, my God, King!" My hands flew to my mouth, and as they did, warm water splashed on our faces.

We giggled, and he wiped his face as he replied, "I mean, we can't go on a honeymoon without having an official wedding, right?"

I couldn't even answer. Staring into those loyal, adorable, romantic eyes of his, I fell in love all over again. I committed myself to him all over again. I even knew that if, God forbid I had to, I would make the same sacrifices for him and my mean-ass daughter all over again. I just leaned over and took the man's tongue into my mouth and breathed a sigh of relief.

For three years, I had imagined how good it would feel to be home, but this was a feeling that I could not have imagined, not even in my wildest dreams.

♪Me, Hennessy & U
Me, Hennessy & U
Me, Hennessy & U
Me, Hennessy & U
U, Me & Hennessy, look what you did to me
I say my head keep on spinnin'
Me, Hennessy & U♪

Chapter One

JADA

Dolla held me until I stopped crying, which took about two hours. Visions of the life leaving Siren's body in leaking crimson blood would not leave my mind. The image had kept me crying out in agony and guilt. I felt like the lowest of the low. Sure, "snitches get stitches." Siren had deserved every bullet that I'd put in her. However, I hated that her killer had wound up being me. I was so hurt by that because I had prided myself on always protecting my family and friends. Yet, I had just killed my sister, my best friend.

Luckily, before I'd made it back home, Dolla had allowed the kids to go down the street to play with friends, so I was free to moan, scream, and cry out as much as I wanted.

As my sobs filled the air, my cell phone began to ring.

Initially, I ignored the call as my cell sat on the coffee table. It was a number that wasn't saved in my contacts. Current matters left me too scared to answer the phone for anyone that I did not know. But when the caller continued calling back to back, I left Dolla's arms, disguised my tears, and answered, "Who is this?"

"Hello?" The caller was obviously taken aback by my attitude, and it showed in her shaky, yet professional tone. "May I speak to Jada Davenport, please?"

I ignored the noises in her background and the sincerity in her tone. I was too engulfed in my own worry and turmoil to even think to pay attention. I just, again, gave her an attitude. I sucked my teeth and blew a heavy breath in frustration. "Who the fuck is this?"

Dolla looked at me curiously. I sensed that his concern had begun to grow the longer I held the phone to my ear.

The female caller stumbled over her words as she tried to talk around my obvious irate attitude. "I-I'm a nurse at Saint Mary's Medical Center. Your name was listed as an emergency contact for Siren Green. Ma'am..." Her pause was full of concern as her words came out full of compassion while I attempted to fight the urge to completely lose it when she said Siren's name. "Siren was...shot...a few hours ago. She's in surgery. You should come down right away."

Surgery? I thought as my eyes darted toward Dolla's wide with unease.

"Shot?" I questioned the caller. My voice was shaking with what she probably thought was fear for my friend, but it was actually fear for myself. "Surgery? So that means she's still alive? Sh–she survived?"

I saw the color leave Dolla's brown skin as I regretfully heard the smile in the nurse's words. "Yes, she survived. I'm sure she'll pull through surgery just fine, ma'am. But please, do come right away."

I was literally shaking so much that I could barely hold the phone in my hands. "O-okay."

The nurse took my inability to speak as nervousness for Siren's condition. She reassured me. "She's okay, sweetie. I promise."

I swallowed hard and forced out, "Okay. Thank you."

Then I hung up before she could say anything else.

"Shit!" I was freaking out! I threw my phone across the room as I jumped to my feet.

"Who the fuck was that?" I heard Dolla ask, but I couldn't even answer him. My mind was racing. I had just shot my fucking best friend, and the bitch was alive to tell it!

"Oh God," left my voice in a deadly moan as gross nausea sent me buckling to my knees. I held my stomach as my head suddenly became too heavy to hold up and fell to the floor.

"Baby..." I felt Dolla's hands on my back. "C'mon. Calm down. You gotta keep it cool, baby."

Hearing the strength and fearlessness of his voice made me realize that Dolla must have been in this situation so many times. How many people had he been forced to kill to preserve the safety of his family and his friends? This was the shit that I'd signed up for when I chose to live this life with Dolla, so I had to get my shit together and continue to ensure that my family stayed intact.

I took a deep breath and sat up. I ran my hands through my twenty-six inches of extensions as if that would further calm me down. "That was a nurse at Saint Mary's Medical Center telling me that my name was given as an emergency contact for Siren." My heavy eyes met Dolla's. I admired that his constant, heavy-lidded, sultry eyes were still strong and unwavering, as if the situation was nothing to cause him to fall weak. It was as if he knew that everything would be okay.

"She survived. She didn't die," I told him.

It was so bizarre that I was both happy and sad to say those words. I hadn't killed my best friend, and I was relieved that her presumed death was no longer on my conscience. But I hadn't killed the bitch! She was still alive to tell on me...to tell on all of us!

"What are we going to do?" I asked Dolla.

Man, if I had ever thought that he was full of shit, and if I'd never believed anything that he had to say because I had caught him up in so many lies, I for damn sure believed him now. Whatever he had to say, I was going to listen and trust him.

"Let's go," he said confidently. "She obviously didn't trick because the police aren't here–"

"What if she didn't tell because she is unconscious or something, so couldn't?"

"She was conscious enough to give them your number."

"Right," I realized.

"So we're gonna go up there and be the first motherfuckas she sees whenever she wakes up from surgery to ensure that she don't say shit."

JADA

Siren's surgery was simple. They wanted to remove the bullet in her back, which hadn't hit any vital organs or arteries. Before we were allowed into her room, the nurse explained that the bullet to her brain hadn't penetrated her skull. Though it had hit her head with enough force to cause bleeding, the cap and braids securing her weave had prevented it from traveling into her skull. It had simply gotten lodged amongst her tracks.

"I'll be damned," I cursed as the nurse walked away.

"This shit *craaazy*," Dolla mumbled as he pushed open the door to Siren's room.

I took a deep breath as we stepped into the room. On the way to the hospital, we had called Meech and King to let them know what was going on. They, of course, had ensured us that they would be there right behind us, and I couldn't wait for them to show their faces. I needed all the backup I could get.

Siren was lying on the bed with her eyes closed. I wondered if she was sleeping until her eyes slowly opened. I thought that she might be still groggy from surgery, until a menacing smirk spread across her face.

"I've spent a grip on weave over the years," she said. "But I never thought the shit would save my life." Then, she chuckled.

Dolla and I stood quietly in the middle of the room. Siren stared at me with a sarcastic smirk on her face, and my eyes were full of a mixture of sorrow and judgment. Dolla watched us back and forth like he was at a ping pong game. The tension was thick and suffocating as we awaited Siren's reaction to me trying to kill her.

"Dolla, can I talk to Jada alone?"

Cool, I thought. *She doesn't want to talk about it in front of Dolla, which means she doesn't want him to know what happened.*

I gave Dolla permission to leave the room with my eyes. He kissed me on the cheek and walked toward the door, saying, "You scared the fuck out of us. Glad you're okay, Siren."

Siren stared me straight in the eyes as she told him, "Me too."

After I heard the door close, I walked a little closer toward the bed and leaned against the wall.

"So what did you tell the police?" I asked her.

Now that the bitch was alive, I was no longer grieving. Once again, she was the snitch, and whether or not she could snitch on me too, I was going to treat her as such.

"I told them that I got jacked. That some local young boys tried to rob me."

I stuck my hands in the pockets of my denim joggers, attempting to appear as if her covering for me didn't faze me. But I was relieved as hell on the inside. I felt remorse for trying to kill her. The guilt was so heavy on my conscience. But the bitch had still deserved it, and my disposition said so.

"Jada, I fucks with you," Siren swore. "You're my best motherfuckin' friend. I would never snitch on you."

"But you snitched on my nigga!" I was heated, but I kept my voice low enough to prevent the ICU personnel from hearing me. "You snitched on our crew...on our *family*!"

When her eyes rolled into the back of her head, I saw so much pure hatred and disgust.

"What the hell is up with you?" I asked her. "Why are you turning on them? What the fuck did they ever do to you?"

Tears filled her eyes as she confessed, "I didn't turn on anyone. I didn't say anything to the police. I swear I didn't, Jada. That bitch-ass detective has been on my ass for years. That bitch is stalking me. She's got it out for King."

My eyes glared at her with confusion as she continued to blow the shit out of me.

"She pulled me over in Meech's car, but it was obvious that she was expecting for Meech to be driving, and not me. She told me that if I didn't want to go to jail, I had to give her something on King—"

My eyebrows curled. "When was this?"

She hesitated before saying, "The night Kennedy had Kayla."

I was floored as my mouth fell to the floor. "That long ago? That detective has been on them all this time? Why didn't you tell me? Or Meech, King, and Dolla?"

"Because she never had anything, Jada!"

"So!"

"I never gave her shit! But the bitch kept pressing, and you're my best friend, so my concern was Meech and Dolla at the end of the day. I knew that if King was gone, we would still be okay. So..." She took a deep breath. Despite the bullets that I had hit her with and the surgery, *now* she looked sick. The color drained from her face as she continued. "I told her about the drop King had to make a few years ago."

My face scrunched with confusion. "King doesn't make dr—" Then it hit me! "Oh my God, Siren!"

"I didn't know Kennedy was going to be in the car!"

"Oh my God!" My white Giuseppe wedge sneakers paced the floor as my face fell into my hands.

"I'm sorry, Jada," I heard Siren say.

I spun around. "Sorry? You're *sorry*? You've been playing us all along! *You're* the reason why Kennedy got pulled over that night! You're the reason why my cousin went to prison!"

"Your cousin?" she asked as she sat up, wincing from pain along the way. "Fuck your cousin! I'm your *best friend*! Where the fuck was *your cousin* when Dolla was throwing them hands at you years ago? Where the fuck was *your cousin* when he was cheating and you damn near wanted to kill your fucking self?"

She was right. She had been there for me for years, way before Kennedy had moved in with her mother, but right was right, and wrong was wrong.

I shook my head in disgust. "You ain't shit."

"I did what I had to do to keep them off of Meech and Dolla," she tried to convince me. "But the bitch kept pressing. For years, she wouldn't leave me the fuck alone! That's why you saw us talking, but I haven't said shit ever since because, despite my relationship with the crew, you are my best friend and I–"

"Stop it with that best friend shit!" I snapped as I raised my hand to shut her up. "If I was your fucking friend, you would have never kept this kinda shit from me! Fuck you, Siren!"

A calm evil came over her that honestly scared the fuck outta me. "Fine," she said with a shrug. "Fuck me."

I nodded. "Good. So what's up? You're telling me all of this now to say what?"

"Because I was trying to get you to understand why you saw me with that detective."

I stood staring blankly at her, my empty eyes telling her that she really hadn't done shit but make me think worse of her.

"But what you ain't gon' do is tell the crew what I just told you because, in exchange, I'm not gon' tell Maria, *that detective that I have in my back pocket*, how you shot me or anything else that I know about King and his organization."

She had me on that one. One thing I didn't want was to be away from my kids and Dolla. When Kennedy was locked up, I couldn't imagine what she was going through. I for damn sure didn't want to find out by sitting in jail for murder, and this bitch had proven that she was just crazy enough to do what she had to do to make that happen.

I hadn't verbally agreed, but she saw the submission in my eyes and seemed to relax, knowing that her secret was safe with me.

"Oh... and convince Meech to let me come back home."

I glared at her in disbelief of everything I had just seen and heard from her. I didn't know who the fuck this bitch was that I was looking at. She wasn't the Siren Green that I had met in high school, who'd fought bitches with me and was more loyal than anyone I'd ever known.

"What the fuck happened to you?" I asked her.

She looked at me and honestly seemed ashamed of the woman that she realized that I knew she had become. Her lips parted, and she was just about to speak when the door opened and in walked King.

SIREN

Dolla, Meech, and Kennedy were right behind King as they hurriedly filed into the room.

"Oh, my God, girl!" Kennedy squealed as she rushed to the bed. "I'm so glad you're okay!"

Before I knew it, her arms were wrapped lovingly around my neck. Since all eyes were on me, I forced a smile. I peeped Jada roll her eyes slightly behind everyone's back.

"Who the fuck did this?" I heard King ask. "Did you know them niggas?"

Kennedy released me from her embrace and sat at the foot of the bed. I noticed that everyone else stayed a distance away from me. Meech didn't even try to front like he gave a fuck about what had happened. Everyone noticed that as well and continued to shoot him curious glances.

"No," I answered as I cleared my throat. "I didn't recognize them. It was some young niggas on goofy shit. I was walking the streets looking like money, and they wanted it."

King and Kennedy shook their heads in disbelief.

"Well, thank God for that weave, girl!" Kennedy chuckled.

I giggled half-heartedly as I watched Meech stare blankly out of the window at nothing.

"Hey, y'all, can I talk to Meech alone, please?" I asked.

Kennedy was the only one that replied, "Sure. You want something to eat? I know you don't want this nasty-ass hospital food."

"Nah, I'm good," I told her as they filed out, leaving Meech standing in the middle of the room.

I waited until the door closed to say something, but as soon as my lips parted, he cut me off.

"You the fakest bitch I ever met." His voice was so steady, low, and calm that it was scarier than him screaming at me the way that he had some hours ago. "You just smiling in her face like you ain't been phony with her for years. You and King, y'all phony as hell."

I tried to give the most sincere face that I could muster, but he wasn't even looking at me. He was still staring blankly out of the window at nothing in particular with his hands in his pockets, appearing broken. It was the weakest I'd ever seen him. As I stared at him, I wondered who had hurt him more, me or King.

But I knew it was King because he loved King more than he loved me. Despite everything I'd done for them, they all loved the almighty King more than me.

They acted like that motherfucka was the second coming of Jesus.

Yet and still, I managed to muster up a sincere, "I'm sorry, Meech. What me and King had was... *sex*, and it was one time—"

"One time you motherfuckas never told me about! I woulda never fucked with you had I known!"

"Then I'm glad you didn't because, despite telling you who Elijah's real father is, I have never lied to you!"

In response, his eyes rolled up to the ceiling.

"Meech, I want to come home. I love you."

He sucked his teeth. "I don't wanna hear that bullshit."

He didn't believe me. He shouldn't have, but I needed him to. I had played the victim with Jada, and though I was sure she would never truly fuck with me again, it had at least bought her silence. But playing this role was not working with Meech.

"Can I come back home, please?" I begged.

He waved his hand, dismissing me. "Hell nah."

"Please?" Now, the sincerity was real. I did have some sort of feelings for Meech. Despite my, what some would call, obsession with King, I did care about Meech and hated that this was happening to such a loving dude. He had taken me and my son in, and he deserved a better woman than me. But I was to be damned if yet another bitch would come and win what was mine.

"No!" Meech spat. He looked at me like I was crazy for even thinking that there was even an option.

Fine, I thought, realizing that being nice was getting me nowhere. "I'm not the only one keeping secrets from my friends," I reminded him. "Let me come back home, or I'ma tell King how you've been setting up your own organization on the west coast."

For the first time, Meech actually looked at me. I was wrong for using it against him because it was something that I had actually talked him into a few months ago. We had money, but being his right-hand men, Dolla and Meech never quite had as much as King. I continuously attempted to convince Meech to use his cousins in California to establish his own organization and be his own "King." He had been taking small steps to put in the work, but he never gave it his full attention because like us all, we were all too loyal to defy King.

Chapter Two

MEECH

"Bitch," I cursed, laughing. "I don't give a fuck what you tell

him."

Siren tried to hide how disappointed she was that I had disregarded her threat. She thought she had me by the collar with that little threat, but what this goofy-ass bitch failed to realize was that I was smarter than that. I had already thrown around the idea with King about expanding my own personal line of product over to the west coast. He had given me his blessing and everything. But with Kennedy getting out of jail, the detectives popping up, and this wedding shit, I had pushed it to the back of mind. It was really more important to Siren any fucking way. I was cool with what I had. My accounts were phat as fuck, and I was living comfortably.

"Well, I'm taking my fucking son, Meech," she continued to threaten. "You can't keep him. You have no legal ties to him. If you don't let me come home, *I am taking my fucking son*, and I know you don't want that. You love him more than you have ever loved me."

Just when I thought I couldn't hate her anymore, I despised her ability to breathe even more right then because the bitch was right. At the moment, I did love Elijah more than I could ever give a fuck about her.

"Kiss my ass, bitch," I told her as I turned around. "Good thing somebody tried to kill you. Now you got a place to stay for a couple of days."

That was some fucked up shit to say, but that bitch had fucked my head up in the worst way. I had never been so hurt in my life. As I closed the door of her hospital room, I felt like I was experiencing a death. Even if King had only fucked Siren once, I didn't believe that he had been too drunk to remember. Siren was covering for that nigga, and I knew it. He remembered, and the fact that my nigga had never told me that shit had my head gone. I mean, if he could keep some shit like that from me, what else was he keeping from me?

I was so lost in my thoughts that I didn't realize I was walking by Jada and Dolla until I felt a tug on my arm.

"Damn, bruh," I heard Dolla say.

I stepped back and joined them while asking, "What are you talkin' 'bout?"

"I asked you a question, and you kept walking by."

"Aw, man, I'm sorry. I didn't see or hear you. I was thinking about some shit."

Dolla chuckled and asked, "Siren got your head that gone?"

Before I could answer, Jada asked me, "What the hell happened between y'all anyway? Why did y'all get into it?"

I wanted to tell them. As far as I knew, these were the only true friends I had left. But I realized the size of the cat that I was about to let out of the bag. At the moment, I couldn't have given two fucks about King's feelings, but Kennedy deserved her happily ever after. The girl had spent three years in jail. I at least wanted her to have the wedding of her dreams without Siren and King's bullshit fucking it up. In the meantime, I would figure out when to holler at King. It was something that I had to calculate carefully because I currently had no respect for the nigga, and you definitely can't make or break bread with a nigga you don't respect. So once this shit came out, it would be a domino effect. It was a strong possibility that our whole organization would fall after this shit.

"Caught her up with some nigga," I finally lied.

Both of their eyes bucked and Jada asked, "*Whaaat?* Who?"

"Better not be a nigga we know," Dolla threatened.

When he said that shit, everything I'd eaten threatened to come up. I cleared my throat, attempting to keep my stomach from turning. "I don't know. She didn't have the nigga's name programmed in the phone. I just saw some text messages."

"Are you going to let her come back home?" Jada asked.

"They talkin' about discharging her already?" I asked her.

"Earlier the nurse told me that she can go home in two days. The surgery was minor."

I couldn't even hide my disappointment as Jada went on.

"I know you're mad at her, Meech, but you gotta be careful how you leave her, if that's what you wanna do. It's too much foul shit going on, and she knows too much about the business to piss her off by kicking her out."

Although she only knew half of the truth, Jada was right. I didn't need a bitch like Siren in these streets with ill feelings toward me. I had to be careful like a nigga getting a divorce with no prenup.

"I'll think about it," I replied as we heard heavy footsteps coming down the hall.

We followed the sounds to see King and Kennedy, along with Brooklyn, who was my cousin and a member of our organization, and a few other members of the crew.

I was happy to see the members of our squad. The more distractions from King, the better. I really didn't want to be around him, but I had been forced to earlier when he and

Kennedy had walked toward the entrance of the hospital at the same time I did. I had been able to blame my fucked up attitude toward him on Siren getting shot, but he wasn't going to keep buying that shit, and I had never been good at frontin'.

Brooklyn walked straight up to me with his hand outstretched to shake up with mine. "What up, cuz?"

I shook up with him as I replied, "Nothing to it," and nodded to the rest of the crew.

"How's your girl?" Brooklyn asked me.

"She straight. One of the bullets hit her back, but no vital organs or arteries. The other one—"

"Hit her weave," he interrupted me with a chuckle. "I heard that shit on the news before I left the crib."

"The news?" Kennedy asked. "It made the news?"

"Hell yeah. That shit is like a phenomenon. Her fucking weave saved her life," Brooklyn laughed. Then he quickly got serious and looked at me. "I'm sorry, man. That shit ain't funny but—"

I quickly stopped him. "Don't trip."

You just don't know how much I don't give a fuck, I thought to myself.

Now everyone was having their own side conversations, and I was just there in the midst of their voices, not really hearing shit because my mind was racing as my blood boiled over. I couldn't stand being in the same room with King, let alone in the same squad anymore, so I announced my exit. "Aye, y'all, I gotta go check on Elijah. I'll holla."

I turned and began to walk away before waiting for anyone's response. I heard a few farewells and comments, but I simply threw a hand in the air as a goodbye and kept it moving.

JADA

"Jada, are you still coming shopping with me later?" Before I could answer, Kennedy's eyes bucked as if something hit her. She stopped climbing into the car and turned around to face me with big eyes. "Oh, my God! Is Siren going to be able to come to Cabo now?"

I shrugged my shoulders and sympathized with her concern for Siren. If only she knew how much she shouldn't give a fuck about that heffa.

"I'm sure she will," I forced out.

"Oh...okay," she said, visibly relieved. "Good, because I don't want shit messing up my honeymoon."

I heard King laughing from the driver's seat of his red Bentley Bentayga. Kennedy joined his laughter, but mixed with her laughter was shame. "I'm sorry," she whined. "I mean, I care about what happened, of course, but my wedding... I don't want shit fucking up my wedding."

I laughed as well as I heard Dolla chuckle while he leaned against our Range Rover a few feet away.

"Am I wrong?" she asked me with a guilty smile.

I smiled as well. "No, cousin. I understand. You've been through a lot. I wouldn't want anything fucking up my special day either. I'll see you tomorrow."

I was so shocked when Kennedy told me about King's surprise while we sat with the crew in the waiting room on Siren's floor. I was even more shocked that Dolla hadn't told me. But it was for the best if he didn't want me to tell Kennedy. Yet, it scared the shit out of me that he was able to keep such a secret with a straight face. It reminded me of times when he'd lied to me about where he was or who he was with. Then I would come to the heartbreaking realization of the truth through a bitch, or his phone that I wasn't supposed to be going through.

"Are you sure you won't be too tired?" Kennedy asked me.

I was beyond tired. A bitch was exhausted. Meech had called me to chase down Siren at the time that I would usually be winding down from a full, active day with the kids and cooking dinner. That was about seven o'clock in the evening. By the time the nurse called to inform us about Siren, it was nearly midnight. Now, it was four in the morning. We had been at the hospital for hours while various members of our crew filed in and out, making sure that Siren was okay. Now I just wanted to go home and sleep the stress away. Luckily, the kids had spent the night at a neighbor's house with their friends, so I could sleep until Jesus woke me up.

"No, I won't be tired," I finally told her. "But we aren't going shopping until at least two o'clock."

"Okay, cool! See you tomorrow." The smile on her face as she climbed into the car was so full of life and genuine happiness. I cared more about keeping that smile on her face than ruining her happiness by telling her who had really sent her to jail. Besides, if I had told her, I knew that Siren's crazy ass would keep her promise of turning me in. There was just no telling what that bitch was capable of, so I was keeping my mouth shut...for the moment.

I climbed into the passenger's side of Dolla's truck just as King pulled off. I was so glad that they were gone. Words had been on the tips of my and Dolla's tongues all day, but we couldn't say shit because people were constantly around us.

"What the fuck are we going to do?" I asked Dolla as he started the engine.

He sighed heavily. "I don't fucking know, but we gotta say something."

I had told him everything Siren had said. Of course, I had. He was my man, and despite his past transgressions, he was the only person I trusted with secrets.

Besides, I had to tell somebody that crazy-ass shit!

"When?" I asked nervously. "Not now. I mean, with the wedding and all."

I was relieved when he agreed. "Right. We can't fuck that up for them."

"You think she'll holla at the detective?"

Just then, I heard one of Dolla's phones vibrate. When he discreetly hid the screen from me as he looked at it, my woman's intuition woke up. I tried hard as hell to see the name of the person who was calling him, but he quickly ignored the call.

"Nah," he answered smoothly. "She wants back in with Meech. She won't fuck that up."

Before I could open my mouth, the phone vibrated again. Again, I tried to see the name as he ignored the call for the second time.

My heart sank.

This was the third or fourth time that he had ignored a call or hidden his screen that night. Someone was calling him back to back at this time of morning, before daybreak, for only one thing. I prayed to God that I was wrong. I couldn't take this nigga cheating on top of the present bullshit, but something felt fishy. However, we had more pressing matters at hand, so I shoved the doubts into the back of mind and focused.

"She was willing to get rid of Meech when she snitched about that murder," I said. "Snitching on that murder was potentially snitching on you, Meech, and King. That's getting rid of the entire organization and the money. Without y'all, she would have had nothing, so obviously she doesn't care about fucking up anything with Meech."

"But you said that she denied saying anything about the murder. If she admitted to being the reason why Kennedy got pulled over that night, why not be honest about that too?"

My head fell into my hands. I couldn't wrap my head around any of this shit.

"I mean, the bitch is not to be trusted *period*," I heard Dolla say. "But we're all still free, including you, so we still have time to figure this out. Not much time, but...we still have time."

KENNEDY

"Where is it going to be? A venue? A church? Outside? No, the weather is too unpredictable in May. It's not that hot yet. You wouldn't do that."

King chuckled from the driver's seat, but I didn't find shit funny. He refused to give me one detail about the wedding, and the shit was driving me insane! "King! Stop laughing at me!"

But he kept chuckling, so I kept pouting, hoping that as always, King would give his queen what she wanted. "*Pleeease*, King?"

"It's called a *surprise* for a reason, baby."

"Tell me something. What dress did you pick out? Who's doing my ma—"

"*Kennedy*," he said forcefully as he slid his hand smoothly on my thigh.

The mere feeling of his skin against mine sent lustful lightning through my body and shut me clean up. It had only been a few days since I was free, so being with him, being near him, was still like new. "I promise you'll have the time of your life. It will be the day of your dreams. I owe you that, so I promise you, that's what you're going to get."

"That isn't why you're doing this, is it?"

King briefly looked at me questionably before having to force his eyes back on the road. "What do you mean?"

"Because I went to jail for you...That isn't why you're giving me this wedding, is it?"

"N–"

"Because I'm perfectly happy with the way we got married—"

"Baby—"

"And you've been literally showering me with gifts since I got home—"

"Babe—"

"I don't need some big lavish wedding to make the last three years go away—"

"Babe!" he shouted as I felt the car come to a sudden halt. I looked around frantically once I realized that we were in the middle of an intersection. Although it was four in the morning and the streets were clear, I didn't need his kingpin ass sitting pretty in a Bentley attracting attention from the police. Once he was satisfied that he had gotten my undivided attention, he released the brake, and we began to move again.

"I know that nothing would ever repay you for what you did for me. But I spent years without you, out here getting money, and taking care of everybody except the one person that I really wanted to. You're back home now, so please..."

He paused, grabbed my hand, kissed the back of it and said, "...let me do this."

I thought I was the one that was spoiled, but King...he was definitely spoiled. He also always got whatever he wanted, because like always, I had shut the hell up and let him have his way.

CHAPTER THREE

JADA

I couldn't sleep much at all once I got home. Everything that had happened had my mind going fifty miles an hour. However, Dolla was next to me, sleeping like a baby. As I eyed him, those calls that he had ignored drove me crazier with anxiety than Siren was.

He had been distant over the last few days. At first, I thought it was the threat of the police showing up or the excitement of Kennedy's release, but there had been something else. I knew it when he kept ignoring those calls that night, which continued until we got home and he just turned the phone off altogether. I was too tired to confront him about it, and I still was. And the present exhaustion that I felt as I watched him quietly snore was not from the drama that happened that day. It was from all of the bullshit Dolla had already put me through, and the possibility that he was putting me through it again.

Don't get me wrong, Dolla loved me, but it took us going through hell, high water, and a couple of natural disasters to get us where we were that day. When we were teenagers, I had to fight every bitch in the hood over him. Now that I was more mature, I realized that that drama came with us being kids with money. However, there were one or two bitches once we were grown, and even as of two years ago, that had threatened the very existence of our relationship...and him...'cause I had been two seconds from killing his ass.

Just the thought made my heart beat out of my chest. I sat up slowly, looking around silently in order not to wake him.

Where the fuck is it? I asked myself, and not even a second later, the flashing indicator light on his cell phone as it sat on the dresser caught my eye.

I slowly slid out of bed and tiptoed around it, towards the dresser. As I reached it, I grabbed the phone and scurried across the carpet and into the bathroom without Dolla waking up. I didn't even turn on the bathroom light, and I closed the door only enough that it was cracked so that I could make sure he was still asleep. Then I sat my naked ass on the toilet and tapped the power key on his phone to make the screen come on. Of course, it was locked, but I could see the indicators on the top of the screen of missed calls and text messages. I wanted to see who they were so damn bad that my mouth was watering, but the password that I'd seen him use and had used previously to go through his phone was no longer working.

"Fuck," I mumbled, as I tried it again with no luck. "This motherfucka changed his code."

I hadn't gone through his phone, something I did every now and then to make sure he was being a good boy, in about a month. He didn't know that I had the code. I had watched him unlock the phone out of the corner of my eye while we were on some Netflix and chill shit a few months ago.

"What the fuck made him change his code?"

The possible answers to my own question gave me a nauseous ass feeling.

****

After trying every numerical combination that I thought he would use until the phone blocked me from trying for twenty minutes, I had to give up. But, as I tiptoed out of the bathroom, Dolla's deception was even more evident.

This nigga had something to hide. I knew it. I tossed and turned, wondering who the fuck she was, until I finally dozed off around six in the morning. When I woke up around noon the next day, he and the kids were gone. He had gotten them ready for school and taken them, all without waking me up.

I reached for my phone on the nightstand on my side of the bed. After unlocking it, I saw a message from him that he'd sent around eight, the time that he usually left to take the kids to school.

Dolla: *You had a long ass night, so I didn't want to wake you up. Taking care of some squad business today, and then I'll be back.*

I sucked my teeth and got out of bed. "Taking care of some squad business," I mumbled. "Yeah fucking right."

As I entered the bathroom with a serious scowl on my face, I shot Kennedy a text, telling her that I'd just woken up and was getting ready for our shopping spree.

Now, I was finally smiling, as I followed Kennedy out of Starbucks. Admittedly, it felt so good to just be doing something as simple as shopping with her again. We had completely taken these moments for granted before, but now that she was home, little things like this meant the world to me.

It meant the same to her too. I could tell. She was just so damn happy. Everything about her was fresh and new. Even the ponytail, Moschino straight leg jeans with matching cropped top, and pumps looked like the latest of high fashion straight from the runways of Paris on her. The smile on her face was so different from everyone else's. It was full of life, energy, and freedom.

"Ooo, we should go to Pearl's since we're close by," she suggested, and I instantly groaned, causing her to say, "I know you're probably sick of that place."

I swear I was. Since King owned the place, we seemed to have found ourselves there at least once a week, when it first opened six years ago. Now we only went about once a month because we had literally worn the place out. "We can go, though," I told her. "I know you miss it."

She smiled to herself as we waited for the little digital man on the pedestrian crossing signal to tell us that it was okay to cross the street.

"Yeah," she said with a smile. "I do miss it. Miss Maddie know her old butt can cook. Her shrimp and grits is the shit. And Tiana knew just how to make my drinks! Are they still there? Please tell me that they are still there!"

I laughed at her excitement. I didn't know what had her happier, being out of prison or marrying King again.

"Yeah, they're still there," I answered with a smile.

"Ooo! Good!"

As we crossed the street toward our next location, I teased her. "King is going to kill you for shopping in here. You know that, right?"

Kennedy laughed as we walked into the store. "Why? What's wrong with Akira? I love it."

"I do too," I agreed as I took a sip of my grande Starbucks coffee with a double shot of espresso. Lack of sleep and my mind continuously running rampant had me exhausted. "But you know his bougie ass would be super pissed if his woman spent anything less than five hundred on a dress."

She chuckled as she picked up a teal, bandaged dress from the rack and waved it in the air. "This one is two hundred and fifteen. He can round up."

I just shook my head.

"For real, though. I'm only twenty–one. King be into that grown man shit like Balmain, Herves, and all that. I'm not into all of that. I mean, it's nice, but this dress is just as nice to me."

"I know. I totally agree. I'm just saying..." Then I shrugged and left it at that.

"I'll make sure to get rid of the bag and the price tags."

"Exactly!" I laughed.

"Speaking of price tags," she began as we casually browsed some new maxis. "How much is King spending on this wedding?"

"I honestly didn't know anything about it until you mentioned it last night at the hospital."

She took a black maxi from the rack, eyed it, frowned, and then put it back. "I thought you were lying."

"No, I seriously didn't know. Nobody told me anything."

"Siren didn't either?"

Just the mention of her name made my stomach turn. I forced myself not to frown as I answered. "Nope. King probably knew that we would spoil the surprise."

"I wonder how long he's been planning this." Then she gasped. "Oh my God! I wonder if he told my mama! I need to call her. She's gonna kill him if..." Her voice faded away, my thoughts drowning it out. Kennedy was in her own world, not even realizing the deceit going on around her. But I knew, and it was fucking me up so much that the mere mention of Siren's name sent my head spinning in fear of her potential further betrayal. Would I lose my family? Would I end up in jail? Would she end up turning in King after all? Would we get locked up and our children just be out here alone, being raised by any ol' body?

Just the thought was giving me a fucking panic attack, and what was worse was that I was forced to put on a happy face for my cousin.

"Jada!" I heard Kennedy snap.

I finally snapped out of it and realized that we were now standing next to a rack of shoes.

Kennedy was staring at me like I was crazy as I said, "Huh?"

"You didn't hear me?"

"No, I'm sorry. What did you say?"

She put her hand on her hip, cocked her head to the side, and started staring at me curiously. "What's wrong with you?"

"Nothing," I instantly replied, standing straight up and attempting to get myself together.

She pointed at me and smirked with disappointment. "You're lying to me."

"I am not!"

"Yes, you are. Look at you! Your hair ain't combed, and look what you got on."

She was right. I had slept on my weave, and when I woke up, I was too mentally drained to curl it. I had grabbed the nearest PINK jogging suit that was on top of the basket and threw it on, despite how wrinkled it was. That wasn't me. I usually put a lot more effort into my appearance when I knew I was going to be in these streets. I was Dolla's woman, and I had to look the part, especially for these bitches that so desperately wanted my position.

I sighed and realized that I had to give her something or otherwise, she wouldn't give up. "Dolla, is up to something. He's acting funny."

Kennedy looked so disappointed. I hated to rain on her parade, but hey, I could have said something way more fucked up. I had chosen the softest blow.

"You think he's cheating again?" she asked reluctantly.

I hoped not. I couldn't take that anymore. And not because of what was happening with Siren. I literally could not take the shit no more! Dolla had put me through enough.

"No tellin'," I said with a tired shrug.

"You really think so?" Kennedy asked. "Maybe it's something going on with business."

I held in my chuckle. Boy, she just didn't know how true that was, but no... "It's not business, I'm sure. It's something else."

"You could be just trippin', Jada! That nigga put you through some shit back in the day. Any sign of bullshit now and your meter goes straight off. Your ass got post-traumatic stress!"

I had to laugh. "Real shit. That's true. Maybe you're right. He's been a good boy for a minute," I admitted.

Kennedy smiled as she added a sexy cover up to the items in her hand that she planned to try on. "Exactly," she told me. "If there is no proof, no use in giving yourself a headache."

DOLLA

♪ *I smoke dope with the riders*
Doors slide when we ride up
Stay inside or get fired up
To live & die in Chicago
Green light it's a go, if I tell 'em to blow
I keep that metal close
That's how we ride in Chicago ♪

I was barely paying attention to the Drake that was blasting through the speakers of my cherry red, Dodge Viper. Usually, I would be amped up, swerving lanes and rapping along to the lyrics because "Live and Die in Chicago" was my shit, but not today. My mind was heavy as fuck. There was so much shit going on with the squad that I couldn't wrap my head around it all to figure the shit out.

Siren was on some of the most deceitful shit I'd ever seen. I hadn't even seen shit like this on those crazy-ass shows that I hear Jada watching, like Snapped and Fatal Attraction. This bitch was some kinda crazy, and she had us so wrapped up that we couldn't do shit about it but kill her. And shit, even when Jada tried to do that, the shit didn't work out to our favor.

It's like this bitch was invincible.

Lock's death was weighing heavy on my conscience. We had killed that nigga for possibly no reason. Siren had denied being the one that snitched about Terry's murder, but until his last breath, Lock had kept insisting that he hadn't tricked. It was a possibility that he was right, but we had killed that nigga anyway. He was loyal to us. He always had been. He was a down ass nigga, way more than Siren had proven to be.

Then Meech was on some bullshit that I couldn't pinpoint. His attitude at the hospital the night before was iffy as fuck. I mean, sure, he had just gotten into it with his girl and kicked her out. Then she'd ended up shot two times. But the way he'd acted toward the rest of us came off shady as fuck. He'd been my dude since forever. I knew that nigga's ways like Jada knew mine, so I knew that something was off with that nigga, besides him learning that he was laying with a dirty-ass bitch. A few months ago, he had expressed starting his own pipeline on the west coast. With his current distant attitude, I was starting to wonder if the nigga was trying to say fuck me and King altogether and do his own thing completely solo.

Then last, but not least, I was on my way to deal with yet another bag of bullshit. I sighed long and hard as I pulled into the parking lot of the Hampton Town condos on Michigan Avenue. Once I forced myself out of the car, I stared up at the building in pure disbelief of this shit. I really didn't feel like dealing with what was waiting for me on the thirteenth floor, but I had to do what I had to do, so I made my way to the entrance.

"Mr. Robinson, good to see you again," the doorman greeted with a nod and his usual smirk.

I returned his nod. "What's up, Stanley?"

"What's up?" he returned sarcastically.

I just chuckled and kept walking past his old, white ass. The receptionist nodded hello to me too, keeping the greeting nonverbal because she was signing a guest in. I used my key to get past the security door and reluctantly made my way on the elevator.

The ride up those thirteen flights was exhausting, especially after the last few days I'd had, but this visit was long overdue. Once the elevator arrived, I stepped out, took a deep breath as I walked a few feet down the hall, put my key in the door of condo 1332 and prepared to make this shit quick so that I could get back to my normal life.

As soon as I walked through the door, I heard the babies crying. Meagan was nowhere to be seen in the living and dining room area of the two-bedroom condo, so I headed to the baby's bedroom, assuming she was there.

I was right. She was inside of the twins' room, standing at the changing table as she changed one of the twins. Alfreda, the nanny, was lying the other twin down in the crib.

"Hey, what's up?" I asked as I walked toward the changing table.

Meagan looked at me and gave me a dirty ass look, which was to be expected. She gave me a dry, "Hey," and kept changing Bianca. Even Alfreda barely made eye contact with me as she spoke and then told Meagan, "I'll give you all some privacy."

As soon as I heard the door close, I told Meagan, "Hey, remind that bitch who pays the bills around this bitch and who pays her salary. She better respect me."

Meagan instantly shot daggers at me. "Maybe she would respect you if she'd seen you more than once! She hasn't seen you since the day you hired her!"

I was expecting this, so I didn't even argue back.

So much had happened in the last week that I hadn't been able to come see the twins, who were born four weeks ago, and I was their father.

Meagan was a chick that I had met at Pearl's about a year ago. I was fucking her on a consistent basis, which for a nigga with a family at home meant about every two weeks. She was a cute junior at the University of Chicago. She had come from a good family. She was smart...no, she was *intelligent*. But not smart enough to stay away from the lying-ass street nigga that had talked her out of her panties. She eventually became my only and steady jump off until she got pregnant.

That shit scared the fuck outta me. Before she got pregnant, she was treating our sex just as casual as I was, so much so that she hadn't even paid attention to a nigga long enough to figure out that I was in a relationship with someone else. I still wasn't honest about the shit after she refused to get rid of the babies, but I stopped fucking her. I just got her out of that dorm and set her up in this condo to buy her cooperation with my shadiness. I figured as long as I was taking care of her, she would back off pressuring me into being with her. My daddy always said, "It's cheaper to keep her," and that's what I had been doing. I'd been keeping her comfortable so she could stay off my back and out of my personal life.

"Where have you been?"

I tore my eyes away from my son, who she was changing. His name was Brandon just like my oldest son.

Fucked up, right?

"Fuck you mean? I told you business been rough the past couple of days. I had business to handle."

"But I just had your babies, Brandon!" I cringed, like I did every time she called me by my government name. "You couldn't find thirty minutes out of your *busy schedule* to come and see them? Gawd damn!"

When I saw Bianca turning in her sleep, I rushed over to the crib to soothe her. I began to rub her back soothingly as I gave Meagan a threatening look. "Stop screaming," I said through gritted teeth.

Her eyes damn near fell to the floor. "Oh, you give a fuck about them?" She was still pissed, but she knew better than to yell again. She was speaking in harsh whispers as she asked, "Where have you been?"

"Aye, you can't clock my moves. We aren't together—"

"And why aren't we? You were good with being with me before I got pregnant—"

She stopped and watched me curiously as I walked toward her. "No, I wasn't. I was *fucking* you. That was clear, and you were cool with that."

She knew I was right, so she didn't say shit as I reached the changing table and scooped Brandon into my arms. Realizing that this lil' nigga had the same name as my oldest son made me sick to my stomach. This would only make things worse whenever Jada found out...*if* she ever found out.

But there was nothing I could do to change this damn girl's mind. She had insisted on naming him after me.

I avoided Meagan's longing eyes as she watched me pace slowly with Brandon cradled to my chest. Even though it was fucked up that they were here, I loved him and Bianca just as much as I loved my other two kids. It wasn't their fault that their father had stepped out on the only woman he'd ever loved, just because he was greedy and couldn't stop fucking side pussy.

"Why can't we be together, Brandon?"

I still avoided her eyes. I had to. Those pretty hazel orbs were hard to resist along with her modelesque height, slim build, and long, brown curly hair that fell everywhere wildly. She had a round, plump booty that gave her the only curve on her body besides that big-ass head. Despite her beauty, she was cool as hell, funny as fuck and super laid back, besides her geeky intelligence.

But despite all of that, I loved my girl, and it took these babies coming into this world for me to remember that I didn't want to lose Jada...not ever.

"Look, I'll be out of country for a few days on business—"

"So you're just going to ignore me?"

I finally looked at her and just shook my head because I saw no love in her eyes for me. I truly felt that she just wanted me because she was used to every nigga being so swayed by her beauty, that she always got what she wanted from them, including their commitment.

"*Like I was saying*, I'll be out of the country for a few days," I reiterated. "So I won't have much of a signal."

"Out of the country?" she asked suspiciously. "What? You niggas goin' to Korea and getting your own dope like Denzel?"

"Huh?" I asked, trying not to laugh.

"You know what I'm talking about," she replied, her own smile forcing its way out, despite her anger toward me. "Like that guy Denzel played in that movie."

"Frank Lucas?"

"Yeah, him!"

I shook my head. "You wild as fuck. But nah, it's nothing like that at all."

She continued to glare at me. She had questions, concerns, and needs, but she had let them all go and was the cool, down ass chick, despite her knowing better, that she had always been.

"Here," she told me as she walked toward me with a bottle. "He's hungry."

MEECH

"Aye, Meech."

I tore my eyes away from the television to give my attention to Tangi, the bartender at the Loca Lounge where I was having a few cocktails. I had been drowning myself in Hennessy all day. It was four in the afternoon, so the hole in the wall in the city near one of our spots was virtually empty.

"What's up, Tangi?"

Damn, it was hard as fuck to keep my eyes off of her titties. She had them big motherfuckas on display on purpose. Those thangs were earning her all kinds of unnecessary tips from me.

"Here," she said as she handed me a shot.

I looked at her strangely and said, "I didn't ask for this."

"She did," Tangi informed me as she pointed at the other end of the bar. "It's on her."

I glanced toward the other end of the bar to see a fair-skinned chick with long, red locs that were pulled up into a high bun. She didn't give me a flirtatious smile or anything. She simply nodded and raised her shot glass. I did the same, and we took our shots together.

"Give her one on me," I told Tangi.

"No, thank you," I heard the chick say, and her voice shocked me. It was soft, feminine, and grabbed my attention more than her pretty face did.

"You bought me one," I told her. "It's only right."

"I've had enough," she whined.

"We don't turn down shots around here," Tangi interjected. "Take the shot, girl. Man up."

She frowned as she asked Tangi, "Can I have some water?"

"Girl, this ain't no water fountain."

"Tangi, please?" she begged.

"We serve liquor. Drink up."

I heard the girl giggle, and again, it shocked me that the sound of her voice did something to me. But I shook that shit off. The last thing I needed was another chick in my life getting on my gawd damn nerves. Siren had my head so spent that my dick hadn't gotten hard in days. But I couldn't help but notice how thick shorty was, and how juicy her lips were as they wrapped around that shot glass while she took the shot.

"Stop drooling."

Instantly, I acted like I wasn't staring at ol' girl and found Tangi staring at me.

"Fuck you, man," I laughed.

"She's cute," she told me softly.

I shrugged as if I had barely noticed. "She alright."

"That's my cousin, nigga. She more than alright."

I chuckled, a blush appearing on my face that hadn't been there in a long time. "Yeah, she more than alright, okay? Damn."

"What's up with you and Siren?"

My face turned into a frown that was so fucked up that it shocked Tangi.

"Damn. It's like that?" she asked.

"Man, fuck that bitch," I simply told her without going into too much detail.

Tangi started to say something, but before she could, her cousin said, "Give us another round, Tangi."

"C'mon on, shorty," I interjected. "I've been throwin' 'em back all day. I ain't tryin' to get no DUI on my way to the crib."

"Blah, blah, blah," she returned, and Tangi laughed.

I looked toward the other end of the bar, and my eyes fell on her smiling face as she said, "C'mon now. We're the only ones in here. Might as well turn it into a party."

Before I could refuse, she left her stool and came toward me.

It's got to be a motherfuckin' sin to wear leggings with an ass like that.

She saw me checking her out, but she acted as if she paid it no mind as she sat on the stool next to me and said, "C'mon, Tangi. Pour up."

We went on like that for two hours. Shorty was so cool that I forgot about checking her out. It was obvious that she was just having a good time and not being flirtatious anyway. We did exchange basic information about ourselves. Her name was London. We were the same age, twenty–five, and she didn't have any kids. We exchanged hair regimens that kept our locs growing healthy, and compared natural hair stylists that we'd been to throughout the city. We were having a cool-ass conversation, so much so that I damn near forgot about the she-devil trying to get back in my crib.

We took back shots until my composure was on its way out of the window, and I was one more shot from having to call somebody to drive me home or an Uber. But I refused to leave my Lexus truck outside all night until I sobered up, so I finally chickened out and refused the last round.

"Alright, y'all," I told her and Tangi as I reached into my pocket. "I'm out of here."

"Booo!" London teased me, her eyes heavy because she was pretty lit now herself.

"Whatever, sweetheart. I'm not trying to die on my way home."

She lifted her hands in retreat as I threw three one-hundred dollar bills on top of the bar. I was in a hole in the wall. No matter how many shots we'd thrown back, London's and my bill combined couldn't have been more than a hundred bucks, but I always looked out for Tangi.

She smiled as she collected the bills from the bar. "Alright, Meech. Good seeing you."

I was tall enough to reach over the bar to give her a kiss on the cheek and a slight hug.

"See you later," I told her as I looked at London and took her in one last time.

I wasn't the type of nigga that gave a damn about a woman's hair. Whether it was natural or weave, I didn't give a fuck. But there was something regal about this thick-ass woman with her locs wrapped on the top of her head.

Again, I just took her in and decided that I had way too much shit going on to add fuel to the fire right now.

"Nice meeting you," I told her as I took it upon myself to wrap my arms around her.

She hugged me back as I heard her say, "Nice to meet you too, Meech."

Damn, is my dick hard? I chuckled to myself as I once again said goodbye and made my exit.

My walk was a lil' wobbly and hazy. *Get your shit together, nigga.*

I took deep breaths and attempted to make the world stop spinning. I forced myself to appear sober on the outside as I crossed the street toward my truck. I made it into the driver's seat successfully and immediately downed the bottle of water that was luckily in the passenger's seat. As I finished it, my eyes fell on the picture window of the bar, and I saw London now standing up and dancing. My dick moved along to every sway of her hips. I had half a mind to go back in and get her number. I literally had my hand on the door handle until my phone rang, and I saw Siren's name on the caller ID. I instantly sat back and started the engine. Shorty was bad, but I was man enough not to put her in the middle of what I knew was about to be some long-lasting bullshit.

Chapter Four

SIREN

"Urgh!" I groaned. "Oh my God! What the fuck do you want?"

Maria was the last face that I wanted to see. I had told a lot of lies and done a lot of deceitful shit, but I was telling the complete truth when I told her that I was not playing this game with her anymore. If she wanted King, she was going to get him herself. Yeah, I wanted King gone. I hated that nigga but loved him with the same breath. But I was also smart. I had played my position with Meech because I knew that he was a good man who loved me and my child the way that I wanted King to. And when Meech kicked me out, I realized just how much I didn't have without him.

I was no longer going to jeopardize what small ties I had left with the crew to help Maria take down our empire.

"I just came to check on you, Siren," Maria told me as she walked into the room.

I frowned. "Okay, so as you can see, I'm alive. So goodbye."

"Why are you rushing me out?'

"Because! For you to be trying to be so undercover, you're doing a bad job. What if one of them walks in here and sees you?"

She rolled her eyes to the back of her head as she got comfortable in the chair against the wall. "I'm a *detective*, Siren. I investigate shit. I know that no one has come to see you since the day you got shot, except your mother."

I hated that this bitch knew every fucking thing. She was right. I hadn't expected Dolla, Jada, Meech or King to come see me, though. Meech hated me. King had always barely fucked with me. Jada, most likely, no longer fucked with me, and she tells Dolla every fucking thing, so I wasn't expecting to see him either.

"What the fuck do you want, Maria?"

"Like I said, I was just checking on you."

"And I also said that I am not helping you with this King shit anymore, so you might as well stop checking on me."

"That's fine, Siren," she retorted with a shrug. "I'll take down his entire organization on my own. I don't need your help."

I frowned disgustingly at her. "We live in Chicago. There're niggas out there killing each other every day, all day. Why don't you go investigate that shit? What's your obsession with King?"

I'd had the nerve to ask, right? Here I was obsessing over the nigga too, but shit, I had my reasons. However, the smile that Maria gave me as she stood up and smoothed out her jeans told me that she had her reasons too.

She replied, "The same as yours, Siren. My obsession is the same as yours."

My eyebrows curled curiously until she added, "He hurts people, Siren, and it's unfair that he continues to get away with it." She opened the door and told me, "Take care, Siren."

I shook my head as she left, thinking, *Crazy ass bitch*.

MARIA

Siren didn't realize how much alike we really were. As I made my way on the elevator, that constant sickening ball in the pit of my stomach which surfaced every time I thought of Damion "King" Carter, was back.

Asshole, I thought to myself, standing in the elevator, attempting to mask my anger so that I wouldn't scare the old ladies that had gotten on with me.

It was hard to hide my hatred for King, though. Siren was right. I was indeed obsessed with making King pay since he had ruined my life ten years ago.

I was eighteen years old when my cousins, Antonella and Elana, had convinced me to go clubbing with them. Elana was fucking this hot bouncer that had promised to let us into Excalibur nightclub despite the fact that we were underage. It was a Friday night, and we were downtown in Chicago. The club was packed, but it wasn't too packed for King, who was standing in VIP, to go unnoticed.

"Gawd damn, he's fine," I yelled into Elena's ear so that she could hear me over the music.

Elana was moving her hips to 50 Cent's "Candy Shop," as she asked me, "Who?"

When I pointed to King, he actually caught me and my olive skin instantly turned beet red as his eyes stared into mine. I should've been afraid of that dangerous glare in his eyes. The massive amount of ink displayed around his wife beater made him look even more treacherous. Every time I thought back to that night, I kicked myself in the ass for not listening to my gut because it was screaming that this man was a bad boy that I needed to stay clear of. Even Elana had tried to warn me.

"Ewe, Maria. You're always falling for some black thug," *she told me with a frown.*

King and I never broke eye contact as I replied, "Don't be an ass, Elana."

"He is cute, though. Fuck, you know who he looks like?"

"Who?"

"That guy who plays for the Orlando Magic."

"Dwight Howard?"

"Yeah!"

I sucked my teeth. "All black people don't look alike, stupid. He's built like Dwight Howard, but that face belongs in GQ."

I began to stare even harder, too wrapped up in taking him all in to give a fuck that he saw me ogling him.

Just then, King's lips turned into a smile that made his bad boy image run away, and a pure gentleman appeared in its place. I broke into a complete beam, and he motioned for me to come over.

"Go," Elana urged. She even slightly pushed me with her hip.

"Come with me," I said, finally looking into her eyes.

"Antonella is still in the bathroom. We'll come as soon as she gets back."

I took a deep breath as I said, "Okay," and made my way over to VIP.

I watched King as he whispered to the bouncer that was securing the area. The bouncer opened the rope for me as soon as I approached him and let me in. I felt like a twelve–year–old girl with King's eyes on me. His stare was intimidating as he checked out my petite frame in a sexy jumpsuit. My juicy 32-D breasts and flat stomach were overly exposed by the jumpsuit's extremely plunging neckline. I knew that black guys loved big asses, so I hoped that King didn't mind my small, apple-shaped booty.

"How you doin', ma?" When King instantly wrapped his arms around me, and his deep voice fanned against my ear, it made my body shake.

I knew exactly what the rest of the night was going to entail.

"I'm great," I answered with a flirtatious glance. "What's your name?"

"King. Yours?"

"Isabel." I'd given him my middle name, which is what everyone in my family called me in order not to confuse me with my mother, Maria, who I was named after.

He immediately offered me a drink. I had drunk with my cousins too many times to count. So I was no punk when it came to downing the Ciroc that King continuously gave me while dancing with me all night.

Soon, my cousins came, and King's friends didn't hesitate to get friendly with them either.

Needless to say, by two in the morning, King was convincing me to leave with him.

"C'mon, ma. It's been a great night. Let's not let it end."

I smiled into his bedroom eyes. Staring up at him was like staring into a gentle giant.

"Please?" he insisted.

Shit, he didn't have to beg. He had me at "hello."

As soon as I said, "Okay," he took my hand and, after whispering into the ear of one of his friends, led me out of the VIP area.

Minutes later, I was on my back in the back seat of his 2005 Cadillac Escalade. King was on top of me hammering away.

There was no passionate kissing or sensual touching, and he didn't even look into my eyes. However, I wasn't let down since I didn't expect any of that. How could I? I was fucking some guy that I'd just met! So I lay there enjoying his emotionless, deep penetration as much as I could, considering the awkward position that we were in.

For five minutes, he plummeted my pussy until he released.

"Oh shit," I heard him say immediately afterward.

My eyes shot open, and I saw him looking down. "Oh shit, what?" I asked.

It was dark in the parking lot of the club, so I couldn't see what he was looking at.

"The fucking condom broke."

I sat straight up. "Are you fucking serious?"

"It's cool, ma. Ain't you on birth control or something?"

"No!"

It wasn't so dark in the truck that I didn't see his eyes bulge. "You clean?"

I sucked my teeth as I pulled my bodysuit back on. "Yeah. You?"

"Yeah."

There was crazy tension between us as we both got dressed. Then, as we climbed out of the back seat, he totally played me.

He was looking out of the windshield towards the club. "There go your cousins. Cool, you can ride with them. I got some shit to take care of."

My eyes rolled to the back of my head as I thought, Figures.

I didn't even argue with him. I didn't expect the man to fall in love with me and sweep me off of my feet. We'd both gotten what we wanted, and I was sure that with his looks and obvious money, he had nights like this every night. I wasn't even expecting him to ask for my number, but he did before I got out of the truck. As we exchanged numbers, I wasn't expecting him to use mine at all, and he didn't for the next two weeks. I was sure that he had forgotten about me, but he was still heavily on my mind. He was sexy, had presence, and he was any teenage girl's dream guy. I was way too stubborn to call him first, though. Yet, life forced me to when I missed my period.

I called King for weeks, but he never answered. I left messages, but I never said that I was pregnant; just that I wanted to see him again. I wanted to tell him about the baby face to face. My parents were extremely religious, and so was I. I wasn't perfect, but I didn't believe in abortion. King and I were going to be parents, and I wanted to tell him that to his face. I had even returned to Excalibur one night, hoping to see him again, but he was nowhere to be found. I called his phone every day for two months, and that smug bastard never answered the phone! I was against killing my baby, but I was also against telling my parents that their daughter was ruining her education by becoming a single mother. So, I terminated the pregnancy without telling them. Elana and I went to a Planned Parenthood after school one day, and I paid for it with allowance money that I had saved up for the procedure.

For years, I forced the whole ordeal to the back of my mind, until I got married. My husband wanted nothing more than to have children, and for years, we were unsuccessful. I was at the gynecologist constantly, trying to figure out why I couldn't carry my children to term. Come to find out, there'd been damage to my cervix created by the abortion that had left me unable to carry pregnancies to term. I had five miscarriages before my husband left me four years ago. Now my ex-husband and Elena are married and raising their two boys together.

To say that I was heartbroken was an understatement. I was mortified and damn near suicidal. I was also mad at King's inability to give a fuck enough to have at least answered the phone. Had he answered the phone, my life would have gone differently. I would've been able to have children. I would've never gotten my heart so broken that I now couldn't feel anything.

Imagine my pure elation when I became a narcotics detective during that time, and King's name came up in one of the investigations. I was delighted to be put on his case because I wanted to be the person that made him pay.

"Hello, everyone." By now, I had made it back to the station in time for my meeting.

Everyone said hello as I got comfortable at the conference table. Around me were a few of the most experienced narcotics detectives on our team. I had developed a new task force to take down my newest, most wanted suspect. At first, I was attempting to take King down on my own, but I now realized that I needed the help of the department.

"Okay, gentlemen," I said as I took a sip of my coffee. Though it was the afternoon already, the caffeine was needed. This was going to be a long night. "Let's figure out how we are going to take down Damion Carter."

KING

"What up, bruh?" I stood to shake up with Brooklyn. I returned to my bar stool as he sat in the one next to me at the bar at my spot, Pearl's.

"What's goin' on, man? Ready for the big day?"

A grin instantly spread across my face, thinking of Kennedy finally getting her chance to walk down the aisle in the dress of her dreams the next day. "I'm definitely ready. Shit, we're already married. This is just a big-ass birthday party for my baby."

Brooklyn nodded in agreement as he signaled for the bartender and ordered a beer.

"Speaking of the wedding, that's what I wanted to meet with you about. Me, Meech, and Dolla are gonna be gone for a few days on this trip. I'ma need you to step up and handle business while we're out of the country."

Brooklyn was from the city of Brooklyn, hence the nickname we gave him. He moved to Chicago to specifically work for us when he saw how his cousin, Meech, was living the good life. Although Brooklyn was only twenty–two years old, in the two years he'd been in my crew, he'd quickly worked his way up the ranks by showing his dedication and loyalty until he was right under Dolla and Meech. He had evolved to making major deals with us, or on our behalf, and made major moves that, besides ourselves, we only trusted him to make. Whenever the three of us weren't available, Brooklyn was our stand in. Shit, even if we were there, he was somewhere in the background. He knew our organization in and out, so there was no one else to run it in our absence.

"No doubt," he agreed with a nod. "You know I got you."

We rapped for about an hour, discussing a few deliveries and niggas he needed to collect some bread from. Then my next meeting came through the door in heels, a form-fitting skirt suit, and a pair of glasses tucked into her long, red hair. Every nigga in the spot stopped in his tracks to check her out as she nearly knocked over chairs with all that ass. She was the thickest white girl that any of them had seen, I imagined.

She spotted me and waved as I told Brooklyn, "Aye, man. I got some business to take care of. We can finish rapping about this later."

As soon as Brooklyn told me, "Cool," Angel was standing next to me with a smile.

"Hey, King."

As she greeted me with a hug and kiss on the cheek, Brooklyn's face told me everything. He looked at me strangely and questionably, so I laughed and shook my head, saying, "This is Angel, *the wedding coordinator.*"

He looked relieved and shook her hand as he offered her his seat and made his exit.

"So…" Angel said with a deep breath. "Ready for the big day?"

"I sure am. Are you, though?"

Angel rolled her eyes. She had been doing that a lot in my presence and, I imagined, behind my back. I had driven her completely crazy ever since I called her six months ago and told her what I wanted to do. She repeatedly told me that weddings like this took a year at least to pull off, but I had been paying her a nice penny to make the shit happen.

"Yes, I'm ready," she answered. "Kennedy's dress has been picked up. The seamstress will be at the wedding, ready to make any adjustments if necessary. The tuxedos are ready. Meech and Dolla got fitted earlier today. The stylists and makeup artists are confirmed. The decorator will be at the venue early to ensure that the space looks exactly how you want it. And the florist will be confirmed once you give me the payment, which is why I'm here."

I grinned and reached into my pocket. Pulling out the wad of cash, I pulled off quite a few one-hundred dollar bills, and she gladly took them from me with a smile.

"She's a lucky girl, that Kennedy," she told me.

"Nah," I replied with a confident shake of my head. *"I'm the lucky one."*

CHAPTER FIVE

KENNEDY

I had married King years ago, but on May 23rd, I finally felt like a bride.

I woke up that Saturday morning to King giving me the sweetest kisses.

"Happy birthday," I heard him say as my eyes fluttered open to the sight of his grinning face.

He was smiling so damn hard that I fell out laughing. "Thank you."

Since midnight, I had indeed had a happy birthday. This being my first birthday since I had been released, all I wanted to do last night was bring it in with King and Kayla. He wanted to bring in a chef to cook us a five-star meal, but I didn't want that. I wanted some good ol' south side of Chicago food, everything I'd fantasized about while in prison. So, we feasted on Italian Fiesta, Harold's and had Garrett's popcorn for dessert. Then the three of us watched movies all night until we fell asleep in bed.

"Breakfast is waiting for you downstairs. The nanny took Kayla down already."

I looked down, just now noticing that she was no longer between us.

I asked, "Damn, I was sleep that hard? I didn't even feel her leave."

But I wasn't surprised. The mattress felt like straight up clouds compared to what I had been sleeping on. I still wasn't used to it.

Seeming as if he saw my mind go to that bad place, King slightly shook me and smiled lovingly. "You ready for this party slash wedding?"

He had succeeded. My mind was off of my dark past and right back on my beautiful present. I smiled dreamingly into his loving eyes and began to play with his dark, curly afro top. "I still can't believe you pulled this off."

He hopped up and straddled me. I giggled as he said, "Believe it, baby! Now get up! Let's get this party started!"

King was so happy that one would think that *he* was the one getting the surprise. That was yet another reason why I loved him so much. It made him so happy just to make me happy. That type of quality did not exist in most men.

Before I could get out of bed on my own, King had leaped off of me and literally out of the bed. He took me by the hand, helped me out, and led me to the bathroom. On the way, he admired my ass in my boy shorts by smacking it softly. I giggled while noticing the time on the clock. It was six in the morning, and it certainly felt like it, but the hot shower woke me up enough that I showered quickly and made it downstairs in time to join Kayla at breakfast.

"Where'd your daddy go?" I asked her, noticing that he was nowhere to be seen.

"He took his bagel and left," Sherrie, the nanny, answered for Kayla, who had a mouth full of pancakes. "He told me to tell you to be ready by seven. There will be a car to pick us up to take us to the venue. Hair and makeup starts at 7:30." Sherrie blushed so hard as she talked. Her happiness for me widened the smile that had been present on my face since I woke up.

"I love that man," I crooned.

"And he loves you," Sherrie added with a light tap on my hand.

Sherrie and I laughed as Kayla mean mugged me with pieces of pancake all over her face. "Aye! What 'bout me? You luh me?"

"Yeah, girl." I laughed. "I love you too. You love me?"

She stuffed her mouth with a piece of pancake while extremely cocking her head to the side, and, I could've sworn, she said, "Barely."

****

My mother and Jada were already in the dressing suite of the banquet hall when Kayla, Sherrie, and I arrived. The smile that my mother gave me told me that she'd known all along, but I barely had time to interrogate her before I was whisked away to get my hair done.

At that point, the time started to fly by. I could barely marinate in the experience. The professional photographer's camera flashed as people poked, pulled, and painted me. Before I knew it, I was standing in front of a full-length mirror, admiring my up-do hairstyle and fighting to maintain the ability to breathe as I realized that King always managed to give me exactly what I wanted. He'd blessed me with the Lazaro sweetheart mermaid gown that I had obsessed over after he proposed almost four years ago.

"I can't believe he did this." My voice was nearly a whisper as I fought the tears that threatened to mess up my exceptionally beat face, but it was hard to hold back the floodgates. Just when I thought this man couldn't impress me anymore, he'd shown his ass once again.

"Unt-uh!" the makeup artist squealed as she dabbed the corner of my eyes with a makeup sponge. "Don't you mess up this paint job!"

"I'm sorry. I can't help it. Look at me." I sighed deeply. "I'm beautiful."

Everyone in the room smiled as I looked in utter amazement at myself. The mermaid gown had a sweetheart neckline with a natural waist in organza, and lace that made me look angelic. The chapel train was completely romantic. The birdcage veil was fierce as fuck!

I couldn't wait until my friends and family saw me. The only people in the room were the photographer, videographer, hairstylist, and makeup artist. My mother, Jada, and Kayla were long gone to get themselves ready with no time to sneak a peek at me before they had to line up with the rest of the wedding party. I had received confirmation via a text from my mother that Siren had been released from the hospital in time to make it.

"It's time!" I heard Angel shouting her announcement. I could see her rushing into the room through the mirror.

I lost it when I saw my father walk in behind her in a white, slim fit Brunico suit.

"Daddy!" I gasped.

"Don't you cry!" the makeup artist threatened.

"Oh my God, Daddy!" He rushed toward me and threw his arms around me as I asked, "You knew too?"

Flashes blinded us as he answered, "Your mother called me. I wouldn't have missed this for the world."

I couldn't believe it. Although we had spent some time together the day I went to his house, so much was going on that we hadn't spoken much since, besides text messages.

"Okay, c'mon, guys!" Angel took my hand and led me out of the room. My dad looped his arm through mine as we made our way through a hall and to a big wooden door. Angel peeked in impatiently, seemingly waiting for a signal. When she finally got it, the door opened and the sweetest, most romantically ratchet song filled my ears.

♪If there's a question of my heart, you've got it
It don't belong to anyone but you
If there's a question of my love, you've got it
Baby don't worry, I've got plans for you♪

Everything was a blur. I could barely see who was in attendance or admire the abundance of stunning roses and calla lilies that decorated the aisle and altar. I could vaguely ogle at the wealth of bling that splattered the walls. As my father led me down the aisle, I quickly smiled at how beautiful Jada and Siren looked in their champagne, v-neck halter gowns. Their thick legs fell out of the high splits perfectly, and they appeared just as angelic as me with their long, full barrel curls while holding the bouquets full of white roses and bling. My heart was so full that my knees almost got weak when I saw my gorgeous, chocolate, mouthy daughter in a Lazaro gown as well. She looked so sweet and innocent with her hair full of bows that I almost forgot how smart-mouthed she was.

♪Baby, I've been making plans, oh love
Baby, I've been making plans
Baby, I've been making plans
Baby, I've been making plans for you♪

Before my eyes could make their way to Meech or Dolla, they found King's, which were streaming tears to the point that I lost it. My own tears began to fall.

The ceremony was short and sweet. After the minister had said a few words, King and I exchanged traditional vows while smiling heavenly into one another's eyes. And then he slipped on my ring. The emerald cut diamond eternity band encased my engagement ring beautifully and made my finger fifty thousand dollars more expensive.

Fuck! I thought as I fought to keep cool. *He gon' get all of this pussy tonight!*

Just when I realized that I didn't have a ring to give King, I felt Jada slipping something into my left hand. It was King's band that matched mine in karat and quality.

"Throughout this ceremony, Damion and Kennedy have vowed in our presence to be loyal and loving toward each other." When the minister began his pronouncement, I got giddy, knowing that I was finally going to be able to put my lips on King. I started to bounce with a smile, and King laughed and shook his head. "They have formalized the existence of the bond between them with words spoken, and with the giving and receiving of rings. Therefore, it is my pleasure to now pronounce them husband and wife...*again*." The audience chuckled as he told King, "You may now kiss your bride."

We received lustful bouts of encouragement from our friends and family as King slowly grabbed my face, and kissed me so slow and sweet that my stomach flipped in anticipation of his sex, despite it being excruciatingly tied down by a waist cincher.

♪It's a beautiful night,
We're looking for something dumb to do
Hey baby
I think I want to marry you♪

That was our cue. At the sound of Bruno Mars coming through the speakers, we reluctantly unlocked our tongues and lips and joined hands.

King looked me in the eyes as he told me, "I love you, Mrs. Carter."

Before we started our journey down the aisle, I returned the affection. "I love you too, and I'm gon' fuck the shit out of you tonight."

♪*Who cares if we're trashed got a pocket full of cash we can blow*
Shots of patron
And it's on girl

Don't say no, no, no, no-no
Just say yeah, yeah, yeah, yeah-yeah
And we'll go, go, go, go-go
If you're ready, like I'm ready

'Cause it's a beautiful night
We're looking for something dumb to do
Hey baby
I think I wanna marry you♪

KING

As she giggled, Kennedy squealed, "You're going to mess up my dress!"

We were in the back of a Porsche limo. The rest of the wedding party was following us in the same kind of ride. It took an hour to take all of the professional pictures, along with all of the photos and selfies that our friends and family wanted to take. Finally, we were on our way to the reception, which was being held in a reception hall in Trump Towers.

I was glad to finally have some time alone with Mrs. Carter.

"Stop, King!" she giggled as she attempted to force my hand away from her pussy.

I had that big-ass dressed hoisted around her waist while I knelt in front of her in my white, Burberry tuxedo.

"Why, baby?" I started to use my thumb to make small, aggressive circles on her clitoris.

She moaned her answer as her head fell back, "We can't, baby."

"You shittin' me. Why not?"

She had no argument. She had fallen into the motion of my thumb. Seeing her pussy cream at my touch got my dick rock fucking hard. "I'm 'bout to fuck this pussy."

"What?" she breathed.

I could feel her looking down on me, but my eyes were on that pussy as my finger slid in.

"Mmmm," she moaned.

"I said I'm 'bout to fuck this pussy. I'm tryin' to shoot this lil' boy up in you."

She chuckled, but I wasn't playing. I wanted my baby boy. I loved my princess to pieces, but it was time that we had a prince.

On my knees, I grabbed her waist and brought her down on my dick. It was hard as hell to fuck around that gawd damn dress, but a nigga like me managed to do it.

"Fuck, King!"

"Yeah, baby."

"Shit!"

"Gawd damn this pussy *know* it's tight."

I started to rub her clit as I held her thigh right where I wanted it with the other arm, and plummeted into that pussy over and over again at a steady pace.

"Fuuuck," she moaned.

I felt that pussy cumming all over my dick. "Gimme this pussy."

"Take it, baby. Oh, yes, King! Take this pussy! It's yours. Mmm–"

The sound of the partition lowering stopped her in mid-moan, but I didn't move a muscle.

"Mr. Carter," we heard the driver call. "We've arrived."

I kept stroking as I ordered with a grunt, "Keep driving."

****

♪She gon' hit the club
She 'bout to turn up
She with her whole crew
And it seem like she ready♪

I instantly stopped in my tracks, looking around for Kennedy. The deejay had been playing a mixture of wedding and birthday songs, and I had specifically told him to play this one because it was Kennedy's shit. So although I was on my way to greet a table full of my niggas, I had to pause just to see her reaction.

"Ooohhh!" When I heard her squeal, I followed her voice and saw her literally running toward the dance floor, hands in the air, as Jada followed her, holding Kennedy's train. When they finally made it to floor, she and Jada danced like nobody else was in the reception hall. They twerked in those dresses and heels and shook their heads as if they had dreads.

I just watched my baby with a proud smile. I was so glad that she was finally the happiest girl on the planet.

♪Happy birthday, happy birthday, happy birthday (bitch, shake!)
Happy birthday, happy birthday, happy birthday (bitch, shake!)
Happy birthday, happy birthday, happy birthday (bitch, shake!)
Happy birthday, happy birthday, happy birthday (bitch, shake!)♪

"Congratulations, King."

I never took my eyes off of Kennedy, but I grimaced when I heard Siren's sarcastic voice. I had managed to dodge this bitch since Kennedy's release, but I knew her crazy ass would find a way to me one day.

"Be nice now. People are watching."

Siren was right. Some of the guests were still eating. Kennedy's mother and father had given their speeches, and so had Dolla and Jada. But many of the guests were dancing by now, while most of them were at the bar. Kennedy and I had been making rounds, speaking to everyone and still taking pictures.

"What's up, Siren?" I asked dryly. "You fix up well for a chick that almost got killed."

"Thanks. Nice to be at yet *another* one of your weddings."

"Trust me, you wouldn't be here if it was up to me."

"We gotta play the part, right?" she asked sarcastically.

I shook my head, trying to hide my disgust for this bitch. Once I had checked Siren the day that I proposed to Kennedy, I thought I had set Siren straight. For a long time afterward, she finally focused on her nigga. I thought she had finally realized that she would never have me and appreciated what she did have. But I soon found out that it wasn't the case. The bitch had actually tried to throw that pussy at me, thinking that I would be weak because my baby was gone to prison. Hell, I hadn't fucked any of the sane bitches that were throwing pussy at me, so I damn sure wasn't going to fuck her psycho ass.

"When are you going to get over that shit?" I finally took my eyes off of my baby and looked Siren straight in the eyes as I waited for an answer. I didn't even really give a fuck if someone noticed the tension between us. This bitch needed to know that she wasn't about to start pulling this psycho shit on me again. "Ain't you got a nigga to tend to?'

"I do," she smiled wickedly. "I just wanted to congratulate you on this wonderful *show* you put on for Kennedy. All of the K&K symbols, the life-sized pictures of you guys, and the fucking white horses; it's all so *lovely* and so *royal*. She's a lucky girl. Wish I—"

I cut her off with a stern glare that clearly told her not to fucking continue. "Don't you even fucking say it."

"What? I just—"

"Aye, what y'all over here talkin' about?"

I was happy as hell when I heard Meech behind me. Within seconds, he was standing next to me, asking Siren, "You okay?"

But it was something up with the sound of his voice. The nigga was being sarcastic as hell, and it was clear that Siren hadn't missed that shit. She rolled her eyes as I noticed the tension between them.

I'd heard through Dolla that they had fallen out real heavy, so I excused myself, telling Meech, "Aye, I'm 'bout to go holla at them east side niggas."

Man, that bitch is loony, I thought as I walked away, but I didn't give her bird-brain ass another thought. She didn't deserve it. This day was about *Kennedy*, and so many people had come to celebrate her birthday and to attend our wedding. The girls had told me how our hashtag, #TheCarterExperience, was trending on Twitter, Instagram, and Facebook. All of our two-hundred guests had social media popping.

If the Feds were to come through the door, the list of indictments would range from here to the fucking Philippines. Every big name in the dope game, from the Midwest to the South and East Coast, were in the building, including my niggas, Omari and Blood.

"Yooo!" I shouted as I approached the table where they were sitting. Over the Fetty Wap that was now playing, they heard me and immediately set their glasses on the table and stood to greet me.

"King, what's up, nigga?" Omari dapped me up as he gave me that one-arm brotherly hug. "Congratulations, my dude."

"Thanks, man. Where's your girl?"

He pointed over to the bar with a smile. I spotted Jasmine looking lovely as usual. Contrary to the dresses that most of the women in attendance were wearing, Jasmine had on a cold-ass, straight-leg pantsuit that had her looking like the girl of a don, which she was.

"You know how she gets down," Omari told me. "She drinks *me* under the table."

I chuckled as Blood approached us. We immediately shook up. "Blood, my nigga!"

I was honored to be in this nigga's presence. Me and Omari were younger cats in the game, but even though he was only in his mid-thirties, Blood was who we considered an old head. He had been in the game for a nice minute. I'd heard that he had recently called himself retiring and spending most of his time with his girl, Tricey. But he still had his hands in some shit.

"Sorry I missed Kennedy's welcome home party," he told me. "Me and Tricey were in Dubai and shit."

"Daaamn! Dubai, nigga? That's that *looong* money," I teased him.

He chuckled. "Act like you don't know that life, motherfucka."

"Right," Blood added. "I heard that welcome home party for Kennedy was off the chain, though."

"It was. Where were you?" I asked him.

"Aye, man," he said as he shook his head sadly. "I wanted to be there, but my mother was sick. She almost died. That shit scared the fuck outta me, ya know?"

I nodded in understanding and left it at that. Everyone in the hood had heard about his ex-side bitch killing his girlfriend and lil' daughter. The shit was fucked up. Nah...that shit was *beyond* fucked up. I could see how the shit was eating him up too. Regardless of his smile, there was always a darkness in his eyes that probably would never go away.

"Hey, King!" I heard someone greet behind me.

I turned around to see Tricey reaching out to hug me. She looked lovely in a lime green wrap dress, some high-ass heels, and that same long-ass, expensive hair that Kennedy swears by.

I hugged her curves lightly and respectfully as she said, "This was *sooo* nice, King."

"Thank you," I responded with a smile as I released her. "When you gon' make this nigga do the same for you?"

As soon as Tricey's eyes rolled to the back of her head, Blood reached for her and pulled her close. For as long as these two had been together, he knew his girl well enough to know when to soothe her.

Before Tricey's mouth could say what her eyes were, Angel came power-walking toward me. She had been running back and forth all day. I had no idea how she was doing the shit in six-inch heels. But I was sure that she knew that there would be money in the building, so she was trying to catch herself a baller in those heels, that tight-ass pencil skirt, and blouse that was exposing all of that cleavage.

"King!" she spat excitedly. "It's time!"

JADA

"Girl, this ring is *everything*!"

I laughed and shook my head as Kennedy shoved her ring in my face for the fiftieth time, seemingly.

"I know! I know! You said that already!" I told her as I swatted her hand away.

She was so elated that she danced in her seat as she slobbered over her ring. She had taken a moment to rest her feet and sat at the table next to me. The kids were on the dance floor with Dolla, so the table was empty with the exception of us.

"I am *so* sucking his dick tonight." The look on Kennedy's face was so full of lust and a happiness that I had never felt before. She was on cloud nine as she stared off into the distance at King as he talked with Omari, Blood, and Tricey. "I'm sucking his dick *all* night."

I hollered with a laugh. "Shut up, heffa!"

She ignored me as she sipped from her drink. "I'ma deep throat that motherfucka."

I raised my hand to stop her. "Shut up, please."

"Gon' make that motherfucka hit the back of my throat."

"Seriously, Kennedy," I threatened.

But she ignored me. "I'm swallowing every last one of his babies."

I gagged. "Would you stop?" I sucked a lot of dick, but Dolla could never get me to swallow. I'm a spitter.

"It's going to be *magical.*" I looked at the dreamy look in her eyes as she stared at King, and shook my head in shame as she added, "I hope he gets my throat pregnant." When I just shook my head, Kennedy finally tore her eyes away from King and looked at me. "You okay?"

"Yeah, I'm fine," I lied.

Kennedy just didn't know the half. She and King were living a fairytale, while the rest of the crew was dealing with a devil in a champagne dress. I couldn't believe Siren had shown up. When she walked into the dressing room of the banquet hall, I couldn't contain my anger. This bitch had a lot of nerve, but I guess she had to save face. It would've been too obvious if she wasn't there.

Then I was still obsessing over Dolla's sudden shadiness and the new lock code for his phone. I was obsessed with knowing what he was hiding.

"Are you sure?" Kennedy asked.

"Yes, I'm sure."

"Did you find out what's been up with Dolla?"

"Girl! This is your *wedding day*! Stop worrying about me and my drama!"

She had a rebuttal, but the deejay cut her off. "Excuse me, everyone, but I have an announcement to make. Kennedy, King would like for you to meet him outside. He has a birthday, wedding gift for you."

Kennedy and I jumped up. You would've thought that King had a gift for *me*, considering the way that I was on Kennedy's heels as I held her train. All of the guests gave us room to get out of there, but they too were on our heels as we made our way through the reception hall, out of the exit, and into the lobby.

As we ran through the lobby, I couldn't help but admire Kennedy's authentic smile. She looked like a kid on Christmas. I admired her love for King and his for her. It was a love that I had never felt, though Dolla and I had been together for damn near three times as long as they had. Dolla and I shared an undeniable bond that I doubted anyone could break. We indeed loved each other, but what King and Kennedy had was a trust and connection that most couples would never experience.

After we burst through the entrance, we ran toward the crowd of people around the valet.

"Excuse us!" I barked as we fought our way through. "Move!"

"Oh, my God!" Kennedy shrieked as she finally made it through the crowd and laid her eyes on King. He was seated on top of the one thing he hadn't gotten her since she'd been released from prison: a car. It was a white Bentley Bentayga, which was a perfect match to his.

Kennedy's high-pitched squeal pierced the air as everyone applauded. We hooted, hollered, and screamed happy birthday as she ran to King. He jumped off of the car and gave his baby a kiss as she tore the keys from his hand.

Out of the corner of my eye, I saw Siren a few feet away in the midst of the crowd, standing next to a stone-faced Meech. Siren was clapping and smiling, but her smile and eyes were full of sarcasm. I forced my eyes away from her and back to Kennedy's smiling face, wondering just how long certain motherfuckers was going to allow her joy to last.

MEECH

"Meech, please?"

I was so fucking irritated. This fucking day was finally over, and I just wanted to take my fucking son...well, *King's* son, home and go the fuck to sleep. As we stood in the parking lot of the Trump next to my car, Siren knew that I was drained. She was begging for another chance despite my obvious exhaustion. She knew that what I had found out over the last few days had me weak as fuck. I was no longer the killer that dared a motherfucker to push me. I was a broken man. The two closest people to me had been playing me for years, and for the first time in my life, a nigga was heartbroken.

She still was wearing the champagne dress that her brown skin and massive curves looked great in. I was still in my tuxedo pants. The shirt was no longer tucked, and it was slightly unbuttoned as the jacket draped over my shoulder. We looked like a couple that should've been influenced by their friends' wedding into a night of passionate lovemaking. Last week, that would've been the case. Shit, if this was last week, I would have gotten a sitter for Elijah, the best suite in the Trump, and would've been fucking her senseless all night long. But right now, that thought just made a nigga want to gag.

I leaned against the car, trying to keep my cool and my voice down because Elijah was in the car. "Siren, I told you. I'm straight on you."

Even though her face balled up as if she was about to cry, I knew that shit was fake. This bitch claimed that she had fucked King one time, but I knew that it had to be more. And the tension between them that I'd walked up on earlier that day had said as much. This bitch was still lying to me, and I knew it.

"I love you, Meech. I really do. I'm sorry for lying to you, but—"

"I know," I cut her off. "You wanted to protect *King*." She cowered in shame as I said, "Look, man, I gotta get Elijah in the bed."

"And *I* want to put him in bed, Meech. Even if you don't want to be with me, don't take my son away from me, *please*." That was the only time that the bitch looked sincere; when she talked about Elijah. If she had been fronting with me the whole time we were together, there was one thing I knew for sure: she loved that boy. I honestly loved him too much to keep his mother away from him another night. He had been worried about her for days. Keeping his intelligent ass away from the TV so that he wouldn't see her on the news had been hard as fuck.

Siren saw me contemplating, so she laid it on heavy. "Please, Meech. I know I lied to you, but it was only *one time*. I swear, I only lied to you one time, and it was for a very good reason."

That was true too. Besides this, she had been a top notch woman. I couldn't have asked for anything more. Shit, that was why it hurt so bad. She had taken perfection and turned it into something so flawed that now every time I looked at her, all I thought about was my best friend with his dick in her.

"Can I come home?" she continued to beg. "You don't have to take me back right now. I'll sleep in one of the guest bedrooms. I just need a place to stay."

I gave in. "Okay."

I could at least give her that. I still loved the woman she was before I found out her secret, and I loved Elijah too much to have his mom out there bogus.

She was relieved, but I wasn't. She hurried and got in the car while I continued to stand there, attempting to get my head together.

"Aye, bruh. You a'ight?"

I looked toward the sound of his voice, and saw Dolla walking through the parking lot in our direction with his tuxedo shirt outside of his pants and unbuttoned as well.

"I'm cool," I lied as he peered into the car.

"Are you letting her go back home?" he asked me slightly above a whisper.

"Yeah, man," I sighed. "She'll be sleepin' in the guest bedroom, though."

Although Dolla chuckled, he looked at me suspiciously. "You sure you a'ight?"

"Yeah, man. Why?"

"You just seem off, my nigga. I mean, I know shit with your girl is fucked up, but is that it?"

"Yeah, that's it."

He nodded, but I could tell that he wasn't buying my story. He probably knew me better than I knew myself. He and I had grown up together. I hated to lie to him, but this was some shit that I had to straighten out in my head before I told anybody...*if* I was gon' tell anybody.

"A'ight, dawg. See you at the airport tomorrow."

I hid my reluctance as I told him, "A'ight. Holla."

As he walked away, I shook my head in disgust. Now I had to spend the next five days and four nights with this bitch. I didn't give a fuck how nice the beaches in Cabo were, nothing would be luxurious enough to help me deal with being around King and Siren. I was likely to throw one of their asses into the ocean.

Just as I was about to slide into my car, I felt my phone vibrate. I pulled it out of my pocket, saw the text message from Tangi, and opened it out of curiosity. Although she'd had my number for a while, she only used it to send me promotional info about parties at the bar. But at this time of night, it couldn't have been anything like that.

As I opened the text message, I realized that it wasn't a text. She had directly forwarded me London's contact card. I think that moment was the first time I'd smiled since I was at the bar with shorty. For a second, I thought about calling her and inviting her out in an attempt to end the night on a lighter note.

"Meech, what are you doing?" Siren's voice pierced the air like a wake-up call.

I bit my lip with anger at the mere sound of her voice. I put the phone back in my pocket. London was a cold piece of work, but she deserved more than to be brought into my world of chaos.

Chapter Six

MEECH

*♪My niggas stack their money just to spend it
'Cause when you die you cannot take it with you
And if you ain't beefin' 'bout no money, then what's the problem?
Don't worry about my niggas, Zoo Wap got 'em♪*

By Sunday night, the whole crew was partying like a motherfucker on the beach, which was the backyard of our villa on a private island in Cabo.

Well...everyone was partying, except for me. Kennedy and King were in straight up honeymoon mode. Dolla and Jada were having the time of their lives, acting as if it was the honeymoon for the wedding they'd never had. Siren was just happy that I had let her come back home. I didn't even want to be on this trip with her, but shit, she was a grown woman with her ticket information, so I couldn't do shit about it.

Like I said, everyone was having a good time, except me.

I was sitting back on a beach chair with my shades on, despite the fact that the sun was going down. Finally, I was in weather that was above eighty degrees. The sand was white. The water was blue. I had never seen no shit like this before.

I had traveled all over America, but had never taken my black ass anywhere overseas. This shit was beautiful. But all I could think about as I stared at King, dancing around with a bottle of 1738 like he had not a care in this world, was how he and Siren had played the fuck outta me.

"On everything, for seventeen, I'm wildin'! Treat my whole squad on an island!" King was drunk as fuck as he and Dolla bopped around on the sand rapping along to the lyrics.

Even the girls were feeling it. Shit, the atmosphere, the music...on the outside looking in, the words that Fetty Wap was rapping indeed described our lives. So I understood their excitement as they jumped out of their beach chairs and started to rap along with the guys. *"'Ziploc gang, bring a lighter! It's gon' be a house party on this island! Shit, boom like M80's on this island!'"*

They were all so happy, while the only thing that had put any type of contentment in my heart was the all-inclusive drinks and the fact that I hadn't had to put a shirt on since I'd landed on this gawd damn island.

As I lay back in the chair, staring at my crew, it saddened my heart, realizing that things just weren't the same no more. For years, I had looked at these people and thought there would never be any betrayal, lies, or deceit between us. But all along, it had been there right under my nose. It sickened me to my stomach when I thought about the day that I had told King and Dolla that I wanted Siren to be my girl. King damn near pushed me on the bitch, and now I knew why. Shit, if he had hit that shit once or a thousand times, he obviously didn't want her because if he did, he would have wifed her up. This nigga had given me his sloppy seconds, his garbage, and we were supposed to be *friends*. Nah, fuck that; we were supposed to be family.

Dolla and I grew up together in the same neighborhood on the south side of Chicago. We played outside together from the age of three until we were teenagers. We went to the same schools together, and had the same teachers and everything. King was an older kid that our mothers would sometimes take in. King never knew his father, and his mother was a drug addict. So he bounced around to different homes until his uncle, who lived on the same block as ours, took him in. Although he lived with his uncle, many of the women on the block took it upon themselves to take care of King because his uncle was a known drug addict himself, who got high off of his own supply. He was just better at covering up his addiction and more functional than King's mother. He got killed during a robbery when King was fifteen. By then King was selling drugs as well, an art taught to him by his uncle. So he lived in the house alone after his uncle's death.

Man...the parties we used to have in that motherfucker and the bitches we smashed were *epic*. Although Dolla and I were only eleven at the time, King would let us party with his crew. He allowed us to drink whatever he drank, smoke whatever he smoked, and fuck whomever he fucked. The three of us were tight as fuck, but as King got deeper in the game, he called himself protecting me and Dolla because we were so young. But once we were juniors in high school, King had a small organization forming that he needed somebody to trust to help him run. He began to groom me and Dolla, teaching us how to be his right hand men, and the rest was history; a history that has turned into my heartbroken and weary present. I was now realizing that our history had meant nothing. No matter how much I had proven to this nigga that I was loyal to him over the years, he had not been loyal to me.

"Meech! My nigga!" King was sloppy drunk, walking toward me.

The nigga was wasted and attempting to walk in the sand in Giuseppe sneakers that weren't making his stride any smoother. I was glad that my eyes were behind dark shades so that he couldn't see the irritation in them.

He plopped down on the beach chair next to me. "Why are you over here actin' funny and shit?"

"Man, that plane ride got me popped," I lied.

"True...true. It *was* long as hell."

When he paused, I looked over to my right toward him and saw that he was staring at the party he'd left in the sand. Dolla, Jada, Siren and Kennedy were still dancing, twerking and bopping to the dirtiest music this island had ever heard.

"Maaan," King sighed. "I luh y'all, man."

I simply chuckled.

"Real talk," he insisted. "I fucking luh y'all. You know I ain't got no family and shit. All I got is y'all. So when I say it, I mean it."

This nigga is wasted.

I rolled my eyes. Not only was I not in the mood to deal with a drunk nigga, but I definitely wasn't in the mood to deal with a lying-ass nigga.

"I'll never let a ma'fucka hurt y'all. I'll live eh'day protectin' y'all. I could never see y'all hurtin'. Dat's my word."

I couldn't help the sarcasm that wrapped around my words. "Oh, really?"

But, again, he was too slapped to notice. "Hell yeah."

He wasn't even looking at me. He was staring off dreamingly into the party. He probably was too drunk to will his legs to walk back over there, or to see me looking at him like he was a gawd damn liar.

DOLLA

"Shiiit!" Jada was squealing as I held her down forcefully with my arms.

I had her in a Kong Fu grip. That pussy wasn't goin' nowhere.

"Yesss!" she breathed. "Gawd damn, baby, you *eatin'* this pussy!"

I chuckled as I realized just how loud Jada was. We were on the beach behind the villa that King had rented for the next four nights. It was four in the morning. Everyone else had escaped to their bedrooms, but me and Jada, being happy as hell to be away from our kids, were still outside cutting up.

"Oh my God!" she moaned after I had slipped one finger in her pussy and another in her ass, which sent Jada soaring. I sucked her clit softly while flicking it with my tongue, causing it to harden in my mouth.

She started to move her hips in small circles, grinding her pussy into my face as I ate her into oblivion.

"That's it, baby," I coached her with a mouth full of pussy. "Let me see that pussy squirt."

She grabbed the top of my head and got hers in, fucking my face. Feeling her clit pulsating in my mouth, I knew she was cumming for me. My finger found her G-spot and landed on it like a doorbell, while I continued to penetrate her ass and suck her pussy.

"*Shat!*" Her shouts ricocheted off of the water a few feet away as I felt her love coming down. "*Oooh myyy God!* Shiiit! Move, Dolla!"

I knew my cue, so I jumped back and watched as her liquids spewed from her clit like a waterfall as she lay back in the sand, rubbing her clitoris and moaning in euphoria. "Oooh! Mmm! Gawd damn!"

I chuckled. "You done now?"

"Yeah," she heaved. "I'm done, baby."

She had made me cum twenty minutes ago. Fucking her dogging style in the sand after hours of drinking and smoking had made me bust in minutes. I was good, but she wanted more, and I wanted nothing more than to please her.

Knowing what she had tried to do for me by killing her best friend, and witnessing that wedding, had me completely in my feelings over her. I had always loved her, but the bond between us had seemingly grown deeper over the last few days.

"C'mon on. Let's go inside." I stood up and then helped her up. Seemingly, her knees were still weak because she stumbled alongside me and was still breathing heavy.

"You comin' in the shower with me?" she asked as we entered our suite through the sliding patio doors.

"Of course. Go ahead," I said as I smacked her ass. "Just give me a minute. Let me make sure that I don't have any important messages."

She whined as she turned and wrapped her arms around my neck. The smell of liquor and my dick was seeping from her mouth, but the shit smelled sweet to me. "*Nooo*! No business. You said no business. This is our first vacation."

"Gimme just two minutes. I promise," I said as I tapped her ass lightly again. She grinned lustfully as I continued, "Brooklyn is supposed to be handling shit, but I just want to make sure I wasn't hit with any emergencies."

She conceded after she kissed me quickly on the lips and skipped away. She was on cloud nine. This was her first real vacation. We were both from the hood, so we were happy with taking vacations to the Dells and Miami. But she had never seen this type of luxuriousness before. She was having a fucking ball, and I wanted to keep it that way. I quickly checked my text messages as I threw off my shorts so that I could quickly get under that rain shower, which I heard running now, with my baby.

I sat on the bed to take off my shoes, relieved that there weren't any messages of importance, but the last text message threw me off. It was just a message from Meagan, which was a picture of the twins. But, for some reason, looking at them made my heart melt. I mean, I may not have been the most loyal man to Jada, but I was a damn good father. Maybe it was the atmosphere, or the liquor and weed, but I was currently feeling like shit for not giving the twins what I had made sure to give my oldest two: *me* full time.

"What are you doing?" Jada's voice scared the shit out of me. I hadn't heard her until I felt her on the bed behind me. I quickly closed the text message inbox as I felt her arms wrap around my neck. "You said two minutes."

"Sorry, baby. I needed to give Brooklyn a few instructions. I'm ready." I stood, eyeing her, making sure that she hadn't seen anything. The smile on her face told me that she hadn't. I breathed a sigh of relief as I followed her exposed, voluptuous curves into the bathroom.

Chapter Seven

SIREN

Although Meech had let me move back in, he seriously had me staying in one of the guest bedrooms. We'd only spent one night in our house after the wedding before we left for Cabo, but I couldn't believe that he had seriously put me in another room! Granted, I *had* lied to him about who Elijah's real father was, but as far as he knew, that was all that I had lied to him about. He was throwing away years of our bond and family over King, and that shit was pissing me the fuck off! I figured that the romantic atmosphere of Cabo would have weakened his heart, but that was a no go. We all had separate suites inside the villa on the private island. Each suite had two bedrooms, and Meech had gone into one of them and closed the door the night before, signaling that I was sleeping alone again. Since we'd arrived the day before, he had no problem showing that he was still disgusted with me. But the fact that he had yet to tell my truth to anyone let me know that our history still had *some* kind of hold on him. But although Meech was being cordial by allowing me to stay, I knew that I had one foot and a baby toe out of the door already.

So early that Monday morning, I crept out of my bedroom and downstairs. I had slept in the nude and I didn't bother to put any clothes on because I was on a mission to get my man back.

Meech had no idea about all of the things that I had done behind his back. All he knew was that I had slept with King once years ago, and now the nigga didn't want to touch me. But fuck that. I had wanted King's heart, but I now realized that I had idiotically risked so much because of my obsession to get it. I loved King, but Meech loved me, and he was my everything. Without him, I had nothing. I hadn't had a real job since I was sixteen and working at White Castle. I had more appreciation for Meech now than I'd ever had before. Kennedy had King. Jada had Dolla. I had Meech. We were all a perfect ghetto puzzle, and I was not about to let King ruin that for me.

Jetlag and constant drinking had left Meech in such a deep sleep that he didn't even hear me twisting the door knob. Luckily, the door was unlocked, and he was still sound asleep as I crept inside. Climbing into the bed with him, I admired his hard body, tats, and mere masculine, goon-like presence. It took losing a nigga to appreciate him, and I was seeing Meech in a whole new light. I had always given him a hundred percent as his woman, but I was no longer willing to lose him. I was no longer willing to give King any more of my attention. King had made his choice multiple times. The final one had taken place as I stood at the altar and watched him marry Kennedy again. I was now making my choice.

Since Meech was sleeping on top of the covers in nothing but shorts, his dick was easily obtainable. It was just as asleep as he was, but as I wrapped my lips around it, I planned to wake it and him up. As I slurped, spit, and sucked, I got excited because I could feel Meech shifting in his sleep and his dick hardening between my lips.

"Mmmm," I moaned as my own lust began to grow.

Meech was a man of pure swag, sexiness, and thug passion. Regardless of a bullet to the back, King, or Maria, I had always been easily turned on and ready to fuck him.

But that feeling quickly left as I felt pain slam against the side of my face.

"Arrrrgh!" I screamed as I jumped back.

"Bitch, what the fuck is you doin'?

Tears instantly fell down my face as I held it. Realizing that Meech had just smacked the shit out of me, my eyes widened with shock. I looked up into his fiery eyes. He had sat up and was looking down on me with a rage I had never seen before.

"Get the fuck out!"

"Meech, are you serious?" I winced.

I couldn't believe it. This man was just loving my dirty draws a few days ago. One mention of King had completely turned him against me so much so that he'd jumped out of bed, grabbed my leg, and was yanking me out of the bed.

"Stop, Meech!"

"I said get the fuck out!"

"Okay!"

"You ain't movin' fast enough!"

My butt was damn near off the bed. I was sure that I would fall and bust my bare ass against the cold tile floor, so I held onto the mattress, shrieking, "Meech, okay!"

He let my leg go, and I looked at him like he was crazy. "What the fuck is wrong with you?"

"I don't give a fuck if I let you stay in the crib, or if you're on this trip. You got limits, bitch."

I was heartbroken. Okay, I know I hadn't been shit to him. But beyond my bullshit, Meech had always been a loyal, loving nigga, and on the outside, I had always been the same companion to him. I was floored that he had come to hate me that fucking fast.

"You gon' fight me?" I asked, baffled and hurt. "Are you that mad?"

"Bitch!" he screamed but stopped, realizing how loud he was. "Fuck you mean am I that mad? You've been lyin' to me for years."

"Meech, I'm sorry!" Each tear that fell was real. I *was* sorry. I was truly sorry that I had allowed King to ruin something else for me. The shit hurt me to my soul, and that pain was coming out in ugly cries.

Meech stood next to the bed looking down on me, his eyes tight with anger and disgust. "Sorry? You got a baby by my nigga, you fucked my nigga and never told me, and you sorry?"

"You're so mad at me that you're treating me like this, but you're still right by his side. I don't deserve the same forgiveness? I don't see you smacking him. You should be fighting him too. He lied to you too! Your right fucking hand was disloyal to you too!"

"Yeah, that's my right hand, but *you* were my fuckin' heart."

The sincere hurt in his eyes broke my heart. "I'm not letting King come between us, and you shouldn't either."

Meech began to pace the floor in frustration. "King, King, King! All you're fuckin' talkin' about is *King*. You're keeping secrets from me 'cause of King. You don't want me to leave you 'cause of King. You're worried about the wrong nigga, ain't you?"

His eyes made me lose any hope that I had for our relationship. I cowered under his angry glare and could barely look at his heartbroken eyes.

"I'ma get you a crib when we get back to Chicago—"

I gasped and finally looked him in the eyes again. "What?"

"You heard me," he snapped as he walked toward the room's patio doors.

"I ain't goin' nowhere! We've been together and we gon' stay together!"

As he opened the patio doors, he shot over his shoulder, "Whatever, bitch," and disappeared into the sunshine and trees covering the island.

JADA

"Urgh! What is wrong with y'all? We're on this beautiful ass beach with this white-ass sand and blue-ass water, but y'all got long faces!"

I chuckled because that was all I could do. Kennedy was right, but I couldn't tell her what was wrong.

"Well, my nigga left me, and I just got shot, *sooo* what the fuck do you want me to do...start twerking in the damn sand?"

Siren's voice had no humor in it at all, and I sensed that Kennedy saw that too. She looked on curiously at Siren, who was laid back in a beach chair next to me with her eyes on the ocean.

To smooth things out, I laughed and added, "And my nigga ain't shit, so what the fuck you want me to do?"

Just the thought of it made me want to find Dolla and throw him in the ocean. Dolla thought I hadn't caught him hiding that phone from me last night, but I sure had. I wasn't able to see what he was looking at, and it was apparent that he didn't want me to see it either.

Lucky for him, I just wanted to enjoy this island as much as possible, so I hadn't said anything about it.

Kennedy rolled her eyes to the blue, Caribbean sky. "Oh my God, Jada. I told you to stop thinking up shit until you have proof."

"I don't need hardcore evidence. I know my nigga."

Kennedy huffed and waved her hand dismissively. "I'm going to get us some drinks. Y'all weren't acting like this last night."

"Exactly. We're hungover," I told her as she left the beach chair.

"You gotta bite the dog that bit you," Kennedy replied. "I'll be back."

I really didn't want to be alone with Siren's crazy ass, but before I could offer to get the drinks for us, Kennedy had hopped up and slowly jogged in the sand in her red two-piece, looking like a ghetto Pamela Anderson, toward the bar, which was a few feet away.

Not even a second later, Siren's demonic voice pierced the heavenly, tropical air. "You're not doing what I asked you to do. He's going to get me an apartment when we get back home."

I didn't even make eye contact with the crazy bitch. I just kept my eyes focused on the ocean in front of us and wished that Kennedy would hurry back with those drinks.

But I did chuckle, saying, "Damn, you must have really fucked up."

I was sure that she had a lot of threatening shit to say, but my prayers were answered when Kennedy appeared in front of us carrying rum punch for three.

She was still wearing her wedding, birthday glow. In her tiny, red two-piece bikini, with beach waves falling from under a big white floppy hat, Kennedy looked nothing like the girl who had emerged from the doors of the Logan Correctional Center ten days ago. She was so high up on her happy cloud that she couldn't see the bullshit going on around her, and I wanted to keep it that way until Dolla and I could figure out the right time to say something, and literally throw the shit at the fan.

Right now, on this island, was definitely not the right time.

As she handed us our drinks, she asked Siren, "Where is Meech?"

"What do you mean?"

"I just saw Dolla and King at the bar. They're on their way to do some excursions, but Meech wasn't with them."

Siren sucked her teeth, and I fought hard to see her eyes under her dark, Gucci shades, but I couldn't. She folded her arms across her chest that was spilling over the neckline of her black, one-piece as she spat, "I don't know. Fuck that nigga."

Kennedy chuckled as she retook her seat on the beach chair on the other side of me. "He's been in a fucked up mood since we got here. I ain't *neva* seen him this mad. What the hell did you do to him, girl?"

Again, Siren sucked her teeth and sighed. "It's a long story."

"Okay...and? We're on a beach with no cell service. We ain't got nothing but time for a long story."

"Right," I agreed only to fuck with Siren. "I don' spent years telling you all of the fucked up shit Dolla has done to me. It's your turn to tell us about your fucked up relationship now that you finally have."

Siren sat there quiet for so long that it got really awkward. We all felt it. So, she finally replied, "Some money came up missing at the crib, and he thinks I stole it." Instantly, I shot her a curious glance, but then I quickly fixed my face and let her keep talking. "Nigga thinks I'm stealin' from him. Mind you, yes, I *do* dip in the stash a lot, but he knows that I do it. But I ain't ever grabbed as much as he claims is missing. I told him that it was probably one of those fucking cousins, nieces, or nephews that he's always got at the crib playing with Elijah."

As Kennedy said how crazy it was that Meech would accuse Siren of this, I replayed the conversation that Meech, Dolla, and I had had in the hallway at the hospital a few days ago. There had been a lot going on that day, but I distinctly remembered Meech saying that he and Siren were into it because of a *nigga* and not over money.

Immediately, my heart started beating with anxiety. It had been proven that Siren had been playing us, but I thought, *What if Meech is playing us too?*

The reason that Siren had just given us was a fucking lie. We would've heard if Meech had a problem with a thief in his crib, even if it was a family. And as I thought more about it, I realized that the reason Meech had given us that day was a lie too. Siren wasn't talking to another nigga. She hadn't in years and wouldn't suddenly be so stupid. There was no nigga that could replace what she would lose if she got caught up, and she was too smart and calculating to make that stupid-ass mistake.

Something was up. Meech and Siren were doing a lot of lying, and I didn't like that shit. Siren's bullshit was now clear, but Meech's wasn't. I started to wonder if he actually knew that Siren was talking to the cops. I mean, they had gone after Dolla, not him.

JESSICA N. WATKINS

KING

After zip lining, Dolla and I took a cab to Casa Rafael's Cigar Lounge to smoke some cigars on the patio.

I should've been chillin'. Shit, Kennedy was finally out of prison, I had just given my lady the best birthday of her life, and I was in the islands with my fam. I should've been content, but some shit was on my mind.

"What's up with that nigga, Meech, man?"

Dolla's eyebrows rose curiously as he sat across from me in a plush patio chair, puffing on a handmade Cuban cigar. "What do you mean?"

"C'mon now, bruh. Don't play. I know you've noticed that nigga's attitude. He's been standoffish like a bitch since Siren got shot. I thought maybe he was just in his feelings about being into it with Siren and her getting shot—"

Dolla interrupted me with a chuckle, saying, "That'll do it—"

"But why be so shady toward all of us? That nigga's been short with the whole crew. He didn't want to hang with me and you today—"

"He was hungover."

"C'mon now, bruh. Hungover or not, that ain't like him. You think it got something to do with him trying to get on solo?'

"Nah. You gave him your blessings, so it ain't that."

I shrugged. "Maybe the nigga wants more."

Dolla shook his head in disbelief. "Nah, man. I doubt it."

"Could be. Maybe that nigga's tired of being seen as my right hand."

"But everybody knows all three of us run that shit."

"But I'm *King*. I head the shit. Even though y'all bosses, this is *my* business. It's my empire, man. Every nigga wants to be his own boss one day."

"But why wouldn't he just do it? Why would he break bad?"

I just shook my head. I wasn't about to keep debating with this nigga because I knew he would forever take up for Meech.

Meech and Dolla were like my brothers, but those two were like *soul mates*. They had grown up together, and their bond was much tighter than what they felt for me. I was a smart enough man to know that they would keep each other's secrets, but I hoped that they weren't so dumb that they would keep their secrets from me for too long.

A THUG'S LOVE 2

CHAPTER EIGHT

DOLLA

By Friday, I was happy as hell to be back home in the Chi.

Cabo was off the motherfuckin' chain. With all of my money, cars, and clothes, a nigga like me had never had his passport stamped, so I had enjoyed myself for the most part. The whole crew had definitely partied hard all day and every night. Shit, I had drank and smoked so much that some of those nights were hard to remember.

There had been some underlying tension amongst the crew that was thick as fuck, though. After me and King's conversation, King continued to look at Meech with a questioning eye as the days went by. Meech wasn't doing anything to make King's suspicions disappear either. As a matter of fact, he was doing everything to make himself look even more suspect. Even though he kept swearing to me that he was cool, it was obvious that the nigga had more issues than just Siren.

Then there was the tension between Jada and Siren, which only the three of us knew about. And then, every once in a while, Jada would cop a small attitude with me. I figured she'd caught me hiding my phone one too many times and now realized that I was on bullshit again.

Shit, the only motherfucker content on that island had been Kennedy.

The tension had been too fucking thick, so though I had a ball, I was honestly glad to be home.

"When are we going to talk to King?"

I blew my breath hard with frustration into my Bluetooth headset as I eased through a yellow light that was turning red. "Man, babe—"

"We have to," Jada insisted. "The wedding is over now. They've had their happily ever after—"

I cut her off, asking, "Now we gotta fuck their world up?"

"And *ours* too."

I exhaled sharply. "Man, this might be the end of *everything*. King had a fucked up conversation with me at the cigar bar in Cabo."

"About?"

"He thinks Meech is on some underhanded shit. He don't like his attitude. I told him the nigga's just in his feelings over Siren." As I approached a stop sign, I tried to shake off the uneasy feeling that all of this bullshit was washing over me.

"Speaking of which, while me and the girls were on the beach, Kennedy asked Siren what she did to piss Meech off and she claims that he's mad at her over some money. He thinks she was stealing from him."

"That's not what the fuck he told us."

"Right."

I shook my head, saying, "That bitch stay lyin'—"

"But wait, though. After I thought about it, I think Meech is lying too. Siren's been my girl forever. I know her. She ain't stupid enough to risk her house and cars over some side dick. She would *never* give another nigga her number."

"So what you sayin'?"

"That I think Meech made up that shit up. And my question is, why lie to us?"

The eerie feeling of even more deception lay over our conversation like a heavy blanket, causing a few moments of silence.

"Man..." I sighed heavily as I slowed down, approaching my destination. "This shit is fucked up. Maybe King is right. But why would that nigga start acting like this? All he gotta do is walk away."

"I don't know, baby, but you've got to wonder why those detectives came to holla at *you* and not *him*."

"True." Just then, my other line rang. I peeped who the caller was and told Jada, "I really don't think it's shit to tell.

Kennedy done did her time. I think she'll suffer even more knowing who sent her to prison."

Jada sighed. "You're right. That's true."

"And if Siren was talking to the cops like that, they would've come knocking on our door a long time ago."

Jada's voice was full of desperation as she asked, "But what if she was?"

"Then she already did, and ain't shit we can do now anyway."

"But we gotta tell, King. He definitely needs to know that she was the one that got Kennedy locked up. Ain't no way she can stay around after doing some shit like that."

"We will. We have to. You're right."

I thought I heard tears as she said, "He's going to kill her. I mean, she was wrong and she deserves it. But you don't know how relieved I was when I found out that she had lived. She deserves to die, but I didn't want to be the one who killed her. She ain't shit, but she's been a sister to me for years. Once we tell King, it'll still be like I had a hand in killing her. "

"This whole tower can come tumbling down all because of some shady shit, and I ain't tryin' to stop eating because of no beef and secrecy." As I hopped out of my ride, I promised her, "I'll figure it out, babe. Just give me a minute. But let me go handle this business. I'll see you when I get home."

"Okay."

I hung up and made my way through the front door of Meagan's building. I nodded what's up to Stan, hopped on the elevator, and made my way up the thirteen flights.

Letting myself in, I was expecting to hear babies crying, smell shit, and lay eyes on an exhausted Meagan, but that was far from the case.

> ♪Milk Marie she got a pretty pussy
> Call it pink 'cause a nigga fell in love with it aye
> She got a thang for me, I got a thang for her
> Never ever let her get away from me aye
> No no, no no, no no, no noooo
> She don't yield at stop signs. Lil shawty on gooooo
> Go go go go go go go get it♪

The lights were low, candles were lit, and Meagan was standing in the middle of the living room in a thong and a push up bra. The bitch was dancing slowly to the Rich Homie Quan that was flowing through the surround sound system that was playing like a ghetto, seductive soundtrack to her hip's movements.

I had to admit it; shorty was *bad*. Even after giving birth five weeks ago, the weight she'd gained on top of her petite frame during the pregnancy had created some curves that only magnified her beauty.

I cleared my throat to make my presence known, and she quickly turned around. The shock quickly left her eyes and lust entered them.

I avoided it and her as I asked, "Where are the kids at?"

Her eyes bucked at my nonchalant reaction to her being damn near naked in heels for me. But I wasn't even trying to have this shit. She saw it too. It was clear in my eyes that I wasn't on that, so she sucked her teeth in disappointment and used the remote to turn off the radio. "Hi to you too."

As I walked by her nakedness, as if my dick wasn't hard looking at it, I asked again, "Where are the kids?"

"They're with my mama." As she spoke, she stood before me with her hands on those hypnotizing-ass hips. I tried to avoid looking at her as I sat on the couch. I tried to think of Jada and my kids back at home. But the shit was hard. Hell, *I* was hard.

"So why did you let me come over here to see them if you knew they weren't here?"

She started walking slowly toward me. "Because it's been five weeks, and I'm ready for some dick."

"The doctor said *six weeks*."

She sucked her teeth and threw her hands on her hips. "Who cares? I told my mama to bring them back in an hour. You have exactly forty-seven minutes to get this pussy."

"Who said I wanted it?"

As she sat on my lap, I pushed her lightly to the side. Besides my dick being hard as fuck, Meagan's audacity was blowing me. I hadn't fucked her in months, so who the fuck told her that I would today?

She smacked her lips and hit my arm, but I ignored her tantrum as I took off my jacket.

"Call yo' mama and tell her to bring me my kids," I ordered.

She sat next to me with her arms folded, snarling at me.

"What the fuck is wrong with you? What did I ever do to you?" she asked.

"Nothing," I simply replied.

"You're lying! The moment I got pregnant, everything stopped. We were having fun. We were good together, Dolla."

I held my head in irritation. This was a conversation that I just couldn't have because she was a good girl. I hated lying to her, but I couldn't tell her the truth. I wasn't ready.

"Dolla," she whined as she held my hand. "What happened?"

"Nothing. I...I just don't want to be with you, Meagan. Why do I need to have a reason?"

Meagan looked at me in amazement. I know a nigga had never rejected her pretty ass or that good pussy before. I probably was the first and only one to do it, but this shit had gotten too deep. I had to stop this shit before I lost my family.

"What are you lookin' at?" I shot. "Go put some fuckin' clothes on and call your mama."

She rolled her eyes and she jumped off of the couch. "Fuck you then, Dolla!"

I chuckled. "You want to. That's your problem."

MEECH

The shit was crazy. I had been on an island with the most beautiful local women for four days. Yet, the entire time, I never smiled. But as soon as I saw London, a smile spread across my face so full of sincere joy that the shit scared me.

Luckily, London nor Tangi saw me cheesing at her, because London's back was to the door and Tangi was focused on serving a customer.

I had just left the spot, checking up with Brooklyn on how things had gone while we were out of the country. It was only three in the afternoon, but I didn't want to go home and breathe the same air as Siren.

That was one pathetic bitch. The way she obsessed over King let me know that her feelings for him ran way deeper than one drunk fuck years ago. She was more worried about that nigga than the two people she should've been giving the most fucks about, which were Elijah and me.

"Damn, mama, that ass is *phat*." I had snuck up behind London and whispered in her ear as I caressed her ass lightly. She spun around with fire in her ass, but it quickly simmered when she saw me.

"Boy!" Her mean mug changed into a big grin encased by those big, beautiful, pink lips. "You were about to get smacked."

I chuckled as I sat on the stool next to her.

"Hey, Meech!" I heard Tangi squeal.

I returned her greeting, "Hey there, Tangi," but I was looking into London's eyes. "How you doin', ma?" I asked her.

"I'm good," London answered in a sexy voice as she smiled bashfully and played with one of her locs. This time there was no bun at the crown of her head. Her pretty locs were hanging low down her back. I liked the crinkled pattern they now had.

The smile on her face let me know that she was feeling me just as much as I was feeling her. Shit, the fact that I was even feeling her was a shock to me. I mean, I was a street nigga in every sense of the word. Getting pussy had never been an issue for me. Bitches had thrown pussy at me when I was broke, so when the money started coming in, I was really taking down pussy left and right and fighting off the ones that I didn't want. By the time I got with Siren, I had been through so much pussy that I didn't need no more, so I was pretty faithful to her. There were a few chicks that had gotten through to me on an off night, but they were just pussy. Yet, without ever having held a sober conversation with London, without even coming close to the pussy, I was feeling her for real.

That was scary, and it made me feel like a bitch. So I shook it off and ordered us some drinks.

After two rounds of hard alcohol, great conversation with feminine giggles, and light touches on my arm, London excused herself to the bathroom.

"Meech!" I looked up and saw a smiling Tangi rushing toward me.

"What's up?"

Once she approached me, she leaned on the bar and stared up at me with disappointment in her eyes. "Why didn't you call her?"

"King's wedding was the night you sent me her number. Then we went to Cabo for the honeymoon. I just got back last night."

"Oh...Well, she—"

A patron cut her off, "Yo, bartender!"

"Wait! Shit!" Tangi shot over her shoulder as she rolled her eyes. "Anyway, she likes you, and I can tell you like her. I have never seen you look at a woman like that, not even Siren. Use the number, fool."

"Did you tell her about Siren?'"

"Nah. You said that y'all aren't together anymore, right?"

I nodded.

Tangi shrugged. "Well, then there is nothing to tell."

"Does she know about me? About my business?"

I had to be careful with that. If London was just some chick that I wanted to stick my dick in, I wouldn't care if she was just some money hungry chick looking for a come up. I would fuck her and ignore any further calls or text messages. But surprisingly, sleeping with London was the furthest thing from my mind. Although my dick grew harder and harder each time she smiled, touched me, or...shit...even *breathed*, I just liked being around her. Just like the last time we hung out, for the past few hours, I had forgotten about every fucked up thing happening in my life while I was sitting next to her. I liked that, and I looked forward to the next time that we would sit by each other. But before I could allow anyone into my life in that way, I needed to know that she would be sitting next to me because she wanted *Meech*. I didn't want her in my world because she was waiting for a new handbag, a rent check, or a new weave.

"She can assume. You wear Giuseppe, Gucci, and Farrago. No man working a regular nine-to-five can afford that," Tangi answered. "But like she told you, she just moved here from Michigan a few months ago. So, she can assume, but she hasn't gotten into the streets of Chi enough to know for sure."

"But you're her cousin—"

"*Third cousin* on my father's side. A father that doesn't even fuck with me," she said, cutting me off and waving her hand in the air dismissively. "She's my cousin and we're cool, but me and you are cooler, so your secret is safe with me." Then she winked and walked away just as London returned.

"Ready for another round?" she asked.

As she sat down, she placed her hand on my upper thigh, using me to hoist herself up on the stool. Before I could give her the lustful grin that was creeping out of me, my cell rang and Elijah's picture popped up. I picked up immediately.

"What's up, dude?" I answered.

"Hey, dad! I thought you were coming home to play Madden with me?"

"I am, son. Give me a minute." As I talked to Elijah, I caught London resting her elbow on the bar with her head in her hand, smiling at me as she listened.

"But you have to *hurry*," Elijah whined. "I have to go to bed soon."

"Okay. What time is it?"

"It's six o'clock. I have to be in bed by eight."

"Okay. I'll be home by seven."

"Promise?"

"Promise, dude."

"Mommy cooked your favorite. It's *pasta*!"

Right then, my heart ached. While Siren was so busy protecting herself and King, she didn't realize that the only reason she was still in my house, cooking and fronting like she was the perfect mother and companion, was because I wanted to protect Elijah.

"She did?" I asked him, pretending to be excited. "Cool! I'll be there in one hour. We can eat while we play, okay?"

"Okay! Bye."

****

But half an hour later, I was on straight bullshit.

"Get in the back seat," I breathed into London's mouth as she kissed me.

When I had gotten up to leave the Loca Lounge, she asked me for a ride to the crib so that she wouldn't have to wait until Tangi's shift ended.

She giggled through our kisses and then she asked, "Why?"

I stopped kissing her and looked deep into her eyes. "I want to taste that pussy."

I did. I *really* fucking did. She just looked like that pussy tasted like apple pie, and I really wanted to see if my assumptions were right. I had spent five days watching King and Dolla get all the pussy in the world, while my dick was too heartbroken to even nail one of the natives who had been giving me the eye while I had moped around the island. The sober Meech wanted to just keep London tucked in my pocket as a friend until I got rid of Siren's crazy ass. I also needed to figure out what kind of shit was going to hit the fan once I decided how to handle King. However, drunk and ready-to-fuck Meech wanted to rod that phat ass out in the back seat of my truck, and deal with the consequences later.

She giggled bashfully and slapped my chest lightly. "You're so crazy, boy."

"I'm far from a boy, ma," I told her. I reached and squeezed her thigh and leaned in closer to her. "And I'ma show you how a grown man eats pussy soon as you get in that back seat."

With her hands on my chest, she pushed me back a little, resisting. "No. First of all, we are too damn big to be fucking in a back seat—"

"We can go in your house."

"It's my *mama's* house and...um...*no*."

I pouted, like *literally*. My lip poked out as my heart sank and my dick cried in disappointment.

She laughed as she pushed me back into my seat further and out of her space. "Second of all, it's 6:30. You promised your son you'd be home by seven. It will take you at least twenty minutes to get home, and trust me, whenever I fuck you, I will need way more than ten minutes."

Listening to my common sense, I knew she was right. More than I wanted inside that pussy, I wanted to be there for my son since his mother and father were too busy being disloyal to be there for him like they should have been.

I sighed, my breath so full of disappointment that it probably smelled like it. "You're right. Thank you."

She looked at me questionably. Her chest was still heaving with lust and desire, like mine. "Thank you? Why are you thanking me?" she asked.

"For caring that I make it home to my son in time."

She smiled as her eyes filled with compassion. I wasn't using Elijah to make her fall harder for me. At the moment, I appreciated anyone that truly cared about him.

She gathered her purse and keys, and when she went to open the door, I stopped her. "Wait. What the fuck are you doing?"

"What did I do?" she asked curiously.

But I had already hopped out and jogged around to her side of the truck, leaving my door open. When I opened her door, she smiled in appreciation of the gesture. I grabbed her and helped her out. As her sneaker wedges hit the pavement, she landed so close to me that we were chest-to-chest. Our bodies touched in ways that I wanted to in the back seat. She placed both hands on my chest, stood on her tip toes, and kissed my lips slower than anyone had in years. There was something different in her kiss. It was longing and compassionate.

"Call me," she insisted.

I think my eyes were still closed as I said, "I will."

"No. Seriously. *Call me.*"

I reached around, squeezed her booty, and gave her another quick kiss just as my phone began to ring. "*I will.*"

I gave her room to walk away although every inch of my dick didn't want to.

I answered the phone as I admired every sway of her hips while she walked toward the house. "Hello?"

"Dad! It's almost seven. You're on your way, right?"

Elijah's voice put me back in focus. I tore my eyes away from London's booty and made my way back to the drivers' seat. "Here I come, son. I'm on my way."

A Thug's Love 2

KENNEDY

After five days in Cabo, I didn't want to do shit but lie in bed and remain sober. King and I had partied so hard and drank so much that I needed a serious detox. He, of course, could not sit still once we got back home. He had left this morning to handle some business. He'd promised to be back soon to lay up with me, and I had promised to be in bed whenever he returned.

I wanted to turn down so bad, but no such luck because Brooklyn was having his twenty-third birthday party at Pearl's tonight. So, I was trying to get as much rest as I could before I had to get ready for yet another turn up. But someone was ringing the doorbell like a fucking maniac, causing me to reluctantly force myself out of bed to answer before they woke Kayla up from her nap. I threw on one of King's shirts that hit me at the knee, and ran barefoot out of the bedroom and down the hall. I flew downstairs and swung the door open without even asking who it was.

Jada's irritated eyes met mine.

"Took you long enough!" she fussed.

"What the hell are you ringin' the bell like that for?" I fussed as I walked away from the door, leaving her standing there.

"I've been callin' you all day," I heard her say as the door slammed closed.

"My ringer is off, girl. I'm tired. I need a vacation from my vacation."

I heard Jada huff in agreement as she followed me into the kitchen. "You ain't lyin'. I can't believe we have to go to Brooklyn's party later."

"I know, right?" I replied with a sigh.

"I wanted to stay in the house all day today to get some rest, but I was irritated. The walls were closing in on me."

"What's wrong?" I asked, knowing what was coming next.

Jada sucked her teeth. "Dolla thinks he's slick. He got up this morning talking about he had to go handle some business and been gon' all day... Here, girl. I got your mail out of the box for you."

I stopped searching the fridge and took the stack of mail from her that she was handing me. "He might be telling the truth, Jada. King has been gone all day too."

As I shifted through the bills, junk mail, and magazines, Jada insisted that she knew her man; that she knew he was on something and she was insistent on finding out what.

"'Bout time," I mumbled with a smile on my face as I came across an envelope and recognized the name and return address.

"What's that?"

I was so anxious to open the letter that I ignored Jada as I tore it open, but she soon snatched the envelope out of my hand.

"Jada!" I shrieked as I reached to snatch it back, but she quickly turned her back, preventing me from getting my hands on it.

"Ooo! *Dre*?" she squealed as I wrestled with her to get the letter. "You got some nigga writing you from prison? King gon' kill you!"

Finally, I got my hands on the envelope and snatched it from her. "Dre is short for *Drea*, dumbass. She took care of me while I was locked up."

She looked at me, her eyebrow curled with sarcasm. "Took care of you?"

"Not like that," I insisted as I sat down at the table and unfolded the letter. "She just looked out for me. Her and Ms. Jerry."

CHAPTER NINE

KENNEDY

November 11, 2012

"Ms. Jerry! Ms. Jerry! Come here! Help me!"

Dre yelled frantically as she held my hand. Since I'd been brought to my cell, I hadn't left the bed, except when instructed to by the guards. When I took that charge for King, I was confident that what I had done was right, but the moment that the door of the cell closed and the guard's key secured the lock, shit got real.

I had no business in this place.

I had been crying for twenty-four hours. Every realization had hit me like the butt of a gun. My daughter was only six months old. I would miss her first words, her first steps, and her first time using the potty. I would miss the first time that she called King "Daddy," and whoever was substituting for me, she would call "Mommy." Some woman would be pursuing the man that I was in here for. She would get close to my daughter just to win him over. Some woman would be out there trying to take King from me, and I was not there to love him enough to ensure that that didn't happen.

That shit broke me down. Every ounce of strength that I had when I walked away from my family slipped away at a rapid, scary pace as I got on that bus, shackled at the hands and feet. My breath left me as I sat on the bus, which was transporting the new inmates from the county to Logan Correctional Center. As we made the two hour drive, I looked out of the window at the street, the stores, and the cars, realizing that I would not see these things again for years.

"What did you do?"

I looked over into the green eyes of a person with the voice of a woman but the swag, personality, and body of a man. She even had a fade. I would later learn, once I was put into my cell, that her name was Drea, but she insisted on being called Dre. She would be my cellmate for the next four years.

She was sitting across from me on the bus, shackled at the hands and feet just like me, but unlike me, she was rough with more tattoos than King and more war wounds than the trap niggas that surrounded him.

I was too busy trying to hold back tears to even respond to her. If I had to spend the next four years with bitches like this, I couldn't start off looking like a punk-ass bitch because I was crying.

"You look like you didn't do shit," she said, answering her own question. "Criminals go where we goin'. Habitual offenders

like felons, murderers, and drug dealers. You don't look like none of that."

I turned my head, not knowing what to say, and attempting to catch the last glimpse of the life that I knew before I arrived at my new home.

But then I heard her say, "You love that nigga that much?"

I whipped my head around. "What?"

"You look too taken care of. A nigga or your parents took real good care of you. So the only reason you're here gots to be because of a nigga. So that's why I asked do you love him that much."

I hated that she was right, so I turned my head to avoid her smug look and returned to watching the city as I answered, "Yeah, I do."

But I as I lay on my cot hours later, fighting for the ability to breathe and praying for the chest pains to go away, I wondered why I loved King so much that I had done this to myself.

"Ms. Jerry!"

Above my cries, I could hear Dre calling for Ms. Jerry in desperation as she knelt down next to me on the bottom bunk of the cots in our cell. She probably thought I was dying. I thought I was dying too, while I lay there with my eyes closed tightly as I rocked back and forth, clawing at my chest.

"What's wrong?" Ms. Jerry's elderly voice filled the room as she entered. Then I could feel an extra set of hands on me as I heard her say, "It's okay, baby. Just breathe. Breathe."

"Ms. Jerry, what's wrong with her?"

"She's just having a panic attack," I heard her answer Dre as I felt her soothingly running her fingers through my hair. "I've seen it happen to folks many times during their first night here."

Earlier that night, as I lay in bed anxiously waiting for the lights to go out so that I could cry in peace, Ms. Jerry had poked her head in and introduced herself to me. She had killed a woman forty-two years ago and was serving life. As she and her boyfriend robbed a black-owned convenient store in 1970, her irate boyfriend had shot the clerk behind the counter. At the age of sixty-one, she figured that she didn't have much longer until her spirit would finally be free. She knew that God had forgiven her for committing that robbery in order to feed her starving children and mother. After starting her sentence, she had given her life to the Lord and was peacefully awaiting death, since she was suffering from stage three lupus and her kidneys were failing.

"Breathe, baby," Ms. Jerry insisted. "Just breathe."

"Can you pray for her, Ms. Jerry?"

Dre's concern just made me feel worse. I felt like I had already lost. One night in that place, and I was already weak and losing it. How would I last four years?

"Sure, baby," Ms. Jerry told Dre. "Lord, in the name of Jesus, we ask you to give this child strength..."

And that was when I realized that although I had lost my family in the name of love, I'd gained a new one.

CHAPTER TEN

JADA

I put all efforts into getting dressed for Brooklyn's birthday party Friday night. I hadn't seen Dolla all day because he was "taking care of business," but I knew that he would be at the party so I tried to *kill 'em*. I wanted him to remember what he had at home, since he was acting like he'd forgot.

I'm a shade darker than a Snicker's bar but with the same immense curves and bumps. Therefore, the orange shorts I picked out bounced off of my skin and showed off my body. My hair was still in the twenty-plus inches of Brazilian barrel curls that I'd worn for the wedding. The loose curls encased my round face and brought out my naturally beat eyebrows, almond shaped eyes, full, long lashes and plump, big lips that Kylie Jenner tried to emulate every day. I had an ass that her sisters, Khloe and Kim, had bought. But my two kids had left me with not-so perky, DD breasts and a bit of a stomach, which was invisible with a good pair of spanx. Therefore, the cream cropped top and cream Giuseppe stiletto sandals that I paired with the orange dukes was indeed killing 'em as I walked into Pearl's.

But was Dolla there?

Hell nah!

The fuck? I thought as I looked around.

Mind you, it was only ten o'clock. Maybe it was a bit too early for Dolla to be there, I figured. When I noticed that I didn't see Meech either, I relaxed. I sent Dolla a quick text message inquiring about his whereabouts as I walked up to Kennedy, who was standing close by the door as well.

"Hey cousin," she greeted me. "You just got here too?"

"Hey, girl. Yeah."

"Come outside with me. I need to smoke real quick."

Nothing but some good weed would keep me from spazzing out on Dolla tonight. I wasn't being soft by not getting on him about his absence all day. The nigga was just so slick about the shit that I didn't have proof that he wasn't taking care of business as he said. Kennedy had been right a few days ago; I did have post-traumatic stress, so sometimes I wondered was I being suspicious because of his past. I didn't want to start any additional drama until I was sure that my suspicions were right.

As Kennedy followed me out of Pearl's, through my peripheral vision, I saw Siren following us with this curious look on her face. "Where y'all goin'?" I heard her ask.

Great. Yeah, I really need to smoke now.

"Jada wants to smoke," Kennedy told her.

Part of the reason why I was so glad to be back home was because I did not have to phony kick it with Siren, but yet here I was; yet again forced to pretend like we were still besties.

Something's gotta give, I thought as we walked to my car. *It's time ma'fuckas learn the truth. I'm sick of this shit.*

And as we all climbed into the car, I thought maybe that night was the night because as soon as I retrieved my blunt from the glove compartment, Kennedy asked, "What the fuck is going on?"

I just looked at her curiously. I glanced into the backseat through the rearview mirror to see that Siren had the same curious look on her face. She asked Kennedy, "What do you mean?"

Kennedy folded her arms across her chest then looked at me and Siren. "I know I've been in my own bubble since I got out, but I'm sensing a lot of tension between the crew. What's going on?"

Just then, I spotted Dolla and a few members of the crew walking up the street towards Pearl's. Suddenly, relief came over me. I checked my phone to see if he'd bothered to respond to my text message.

I answered Kennedy, "Nothing that I know of."

"Right," Siren added.

Then I saw a text from Dolla in response to mine saying that he was minutes away. I relaxed a little bit more. *Maybe I am trippin'.*

"That's some bullshit," Kennedy argued. "If nothing is going on, then why isn't Meech here? He's missing his own cousin's party?"

"He's with Elijah," Siren added. "He was too tired from the trip."

Kennedy still sat with her arms folded, knowing that something still wasn't right. "Y'all not lying to me, are y'all? Did something happen while I was locked up?"

Damn, this shit was heavy as hell on my conscience. I couldn't take the look in Kennedy's eyes. She was seriously concerned and seriously deserved to know. Her wedding was over. The honeymoon was a success. It was time to tell the truth.

I sighed heavily, not knowing what to say, just as her cell phone rang.

"Hello...I'm outside, babe... Okay. Here I come." She hung up and told us, "I gotta go. It's some people inside that still haven't seen me since I got out."

I nodded towards her as I hit the blunt. As she got out, she still had an apprehensive look on her face. I could tell that she still sensed that something wasn't right. Once she closed the passenger door, I let out a big sigh, forgetting that Siren was even in the car until I heard her say, "Bitch, don't play with me."

I instantly snapped my neck towards the backseat and was faced with the barrel of a nine millimeter.

When my eyes bucked, she smirked and said, "Yeah, I carry one of these with me since ma'fuckas wanna shoot me and shit."

I didn't say a word. I just hit the blunt, stared into her eyes, and let this heffa play hard as she continued to point the gun at me. "I saw you looking like you wanted to tell Kennedy the truth. Don't play with me, Jada. That secret is supposed to be between you and me. If you tell it, I'ma lose everything and I ain't having that."

This bitch is postal, I thought as I snatched that fucking gun out of her hand! "Bitch, gimme this shit!"

I was able to snatch it from her hands with ease. Why? Because the bitch wasn't going to shoot me. If she was phony with everybody else, I was probably the one person she truly fucked with. She wasn't sincere with me because she was my friend either. Now that I had learned how spiteful the bitch was, I felt like she fucked with me because she felt no competition with me and she didn't want anything from me.

"You ain't 'bout that life," I snapped. "Fuck is wrong with you?" I asked as I sat back in the driver's seat, hitting the blunt with the gun in my lap.

She really wasn't. She had never even shot a fucking gun, but me? I had rode alongside Dolla in a many drive-bys when we were kids.

I heard Siren sigh and had absolutely no pity for the remorse that I heard in her voice. *Now* the bitch wanted to play the victim when she was just trying to play cowboys and Indians.

Fuck outta here. I can't deal with this bipolar shit, I thought as I hit the blunt hard.

"You can't say shit, Jada," she begged. "I told you because, as my best friend, I wanted you to know everything so you can trust me. I fucks with you. I never said shit else to the cops and I won't. But please, you *cannot* tell Kennedy what I did. It's going to change everything. I've kept your secrets. Please keep mine."

I shot a cynical glare out of the driver's side window as smoke poured from my nose. This bitch had a lot of nerve. Me attempting to fuck around on Dolla on some get back shit, with no luck, was nothing in comparison to her secrets. But I sat there quietly, letting her think that I was eating the bullshit that she was feeding me.

When I heard her say, "Let me hit that," I 'bout fucking lost it. I looked back at that heffa like she had three heads.

She sucked her teeth, saying, "Fine, Jada," as she reached for the doorknob. "I know you're mad at me right now. But you gon' forgive me one day. We're besties, bitch. Always will be."

I continued to look at her like she was batshit crazy as she climbed out.

After she closed the door, I shook my head as I held my face. I had to be in the fucking twilight zone because this *couldn't* be life.

DOLLA

God must have been on schedule to grant a ghetto blessing the next day because He had definitely saved me.

"Where you goin'?" Jada was on the couch looking at me with the same suspicious look that she'd been giving me for the past few days. I had seen that look a few times in the past, so I knew what it meant. She knew I was up to something.

Shit, I thought as my heart started to beat out of control in my chest. I knew the time was coming. *I have to tell her about the babies.*

But right then wasn't the time. On that beautiful, Saturday evening, I was not about to turn my life into an ugly-ass nightmare.

"I'm just going to meet with a buyer, baby," I told her as I headed for the front door.

"You've been handling a lot of business lately," she muttered as she stared at a rerun of "Being Mary Jane."

Even though I was staring at her with my hand on the doorknob, she wouldn't even look at me as she held that judgmental look on her face.

"The business ain't gon' run itself. You know that."

Her snarl just deepened as she sighed and replied, "Whatever."

I simply walked out. There was no use in making the shit worse. I actually was going to meet a buyer, but I knew that my suspect behavior had her questioning everything I said, so I just left. I asked myself when the fuck would it be a good time to ruin both of our lives. This shit was going to crush her. It was going to break her heart, and breaking her heart was going to break me. At the end of the day, I knew that my dick had gotten me into this shit. I had purposely chosen to cheat on the woman that I loved, but I would never purposely break her heart. Not only had I cheated, but I had also created kids with my side bitch. It was the biggest mistake of my life. That was the ultimate betrayal that I just wasn't ready to tell her about, but as I recognized the car that was slowing down in front of my crib, I knew that I had to get ready to tell her soon.

"Oh shit!" I breathed as I rushed toward Meagan's Mustang.

All I could think to do was to get her the fuck away from my house before Jada got a hunch to look out of that living room window. But I couldn't get to that car as fast as I wanted to. My legs were so fucking weak with fear that they wouldn't move as fast as I wanted them to.

Yet, just as she turned off the engine, I grabbed the door handle of the passenger's side door, ripped it open before, and hopped in before she could get out.

"What the fuck are you doing here?" I spat as soon as I got in and slammed the door. But before she could open her mouth, my anger cut her off. "How the fuck do you even know where I live?"

"Exactly! I thought you lived in that condo in Hyde Park!"

My eyes shut with grief as I tried desperately to come up with the right words to say to get her away from my crib. But I couldn't even think straight!

I knew this shit wasn't over when I'd left her crib yesterday. I had hurt her feelings when I shut her down, and as I spent time with the twins, I could see the frustration and wonder in her face. I knew she wasn't ready to let that shit go, but I would have never thought that she would go to this much of an extreme.

"I do," I finally lied. "That's one of my cribs."

It wasn't that much of a lie. The condo she was referring to was one of my properties that was currently empty because a tenant had moved out, and I hadn't even had time to focus on putting another one in it.

"Okay. So what's this?" she asked, pointing toward my house.

"It—"

She cut me off as she snatched an envelope from the dashboard and slammed it into my lap. "Before you even try to lie, you might want to stop leaving mail at my house."

I quickly picked up the envelope and noticed that it was the ComEd bill that I had stuffed into my back pocket yesterday so that I would remember to pay it. It must've fallen out of my pocket while I was at her crib.

"That's not your fucking business!" I snapped to hide my deceit. "We are *not* together!"

"And why aren't we?"

I groaned out loud. "Man, Meagan. You gotta go. You're makin' me late for a meeting with this shit!"

"*No!*" When she screamed, I prayed to God that it wasn't loud enough to be heard outside of the car and inside of my house. "I have two kids that I wasn't even planning on having because I was fucking with you! And apparently you been playing me the whole fucking time!"

I sighed as I saw the tears in her eyes.

What the fuck have I done?

I felt like an asshole. She was a good girl. She didn't deserve this shit and neither did Jada.

"Man, look," I told her softly. "I'm sorry. I'll talk to you about this later." When I added, "Tonight," it seemed as if I had won her over for the moment. "After my meeting, I'll come over and we can see how to make this work."

She sat there with tears streaming down her face, staring at my house.

"You makin' me late, ma. I can't miss out on no money if you want me to continue to take care of you and the kids."

My sincerity was winning her over even more. To lay it on even thicker, I leaned over and kissed her cheek while I took it upon myself to start her car.

I squeezed her thigh and I said, "I'll see you later. Okay?"

"Okay," she said softly.

When she put her hands on the steering wheel, I felt like it was safe to get out, so I did. But I stood at the curb until she pulled off. I sighed heavily with relief as she finally did and said a quick, "Thank God," for Him sending me outside when he did.

I knew this wasn't over, though. It wasn't going to be until I figured out when to man up and break my baby's heart.

SIREN

"You're leaving again?"

Meech totally ignored me. He kept getting dressed as if I wasn't standing in his doorway. To him, I was invisible.

I sighed, simmering in the fact that I had fucked up so much that this man hated me. I could see the hate spewing from his eyes as he checked himself out in the full-length mirror on the wall near the bed that I used to share with him.

"Meech, would you please talk to me?"

He hadn't said much to me since we had returned from Cabo. He would only spit a few words at me whenever Elijah was around, in order to keep Elijah from knowing that he was mad at his mommy.

"You want me to talk to you?" he finally asked with venom in his voice that scared me. "Bet. Dolla has a condo available. I'm gon' holla at him about you moving in th—"

"I'm not going anywhere, Meech."

"You don't have a choice."

"We can fix this," I insisted.

I wanted to go to him, but I was too fucking scared to even enter the room.

He looked at me like I was a fool for thinking this could be fixed. He grabbed his keys and walked by me like I wasn't the same woman he had loved for so many years. He had lost all interest in me, and it wasn't just because I had lied about who Elijah's father was. Besides the obvious hurt and anger he had in his heart for me and King, I saw something else.

When he came into the house last night, there was a smile on his face that I hadn't seen in days. Then, all day today, he had been in his phone, smiling like a little boy...a little boy with a *crush*.

I wasn't about to lose him because of King, and I for damn sure wasn't about to lose him to a new bitch. The last nigga that I had loved chose another bitch over me time and time again. I was not about to allow Meech to do the same.

So, as soon as I heard him leaving out of the garage, I threw on my shoes, ran to my car, jumped in, and followed him. I knew he had been texting a bitch all day, so I was sure that he was on his way to her. If I was right, I was going to figure out how to put an end to whatever they thought they had going on.

Luckily, by the time I sped down the street, I was able to tail Meech. I followed him all the way to the city to this spot called the Loca Lounge, where I'd hung out with him a few times over the years. Since it had a big picture window, I was able to park down the street, walk across the street from the bar, and stand in the shadows as I tried to find him in the Saturday night crowd of the club.

It was easy to spot Meech's dreads amongst the crowd. He was wrapping his arms around a thick, redbone who had red dreads that were longer than Meech's. When Meech grabbed her booty as they hugged and she kissed him on the mouth slowly and passionately, my heart dropped.

I attempted to pick it up as I walked away. I was determined to get rid of this bitch, but tonight wasn't the time. He would embarrass me in front of the entire club, lock me out of the house, and I would lose all chances of getting him back.

But trust, I was not about to lose Meech; not because of King, and definitely not because of that bitch.

MARIA

The task force that I had put together to take King down was doing a wonderful job. We had spent countless hours gathering evidence on everyone in his organization. King, Meech, and Dolla were so high up on the totem pole that they never touched anything illegal. They had their money tied up in restaurants and real estate, keeping it clean. Yet, all I needed was one suspect that was willing to give King up in exchange for freedom. I had gone about that the wrong way with Siren. She was way too emotionally invested in that organization to do what I needed her to do, and I had nothing to use against her that would hold up in court. I needed someone who wasn't as close to the heads of the organization with so much evidence on them that they were facing lots of time. A person like that wouldn't think twice about setting King up in exchange for freedom.

And I believed I finally had the right person.

"Good evening, gentlemen," I said as I sat at the head of the conference table. Of course, a cup of coffee was in hand. I was so obsessed with taking King down that there was no time for sleep. "So what are the updates?"

Detective Miller spoke first. "Transcripts from the undercover cop's wire indicate that the subject is heavily involved in the Carter organization. He was making a deal with the buyer for a large amount of cocaine. They were setting up a time and place for the drop."

I couldn't have been more pleased. The smile on my face said it all. Things were working out beautifully. The undercover cop had been able to infiltrate King's organization smoothly. We'd offered another dealer a reduction on his pending sentence if he would arrange for our undercover to buy from someone in the Carter organization. It took a lot of convincing from the dealer, but luckily, the suspect had accepted the undercover cop's offer while King was in Cabo.

"When is it supposed to take place?" I asked.

"In a few days."

Perfect, I thought.

My mouth began to water with anticipation of finally coming close to taking everything away from King just as he had done to me. I had been waiting to find the perfect person to do it, and it sounded like redemption was coming to me by way of this new suspect, Bradley Anderson, known on the streets as Brooklyn.

Chapter Eleven

DOLLA

"Shit!" I freaked out as my eyes adjusted to my surroundings. Then I realized that I had fallen asleep at Meagan's crib. "Fuck!"

My curses and quick movements woke up Meagan, who was next to me on the couch.

"What's wrong?" she asked. She looked at me like I was crazy as I scrambled to collect my phones and keys.

"I gotta go," was all that I said.

Meagan was still looking at me strangely upside my head as she asked, "Why?"

After I got her to get away from my crib last night, I'd kept my promise and come to her condo. She had dinner and a drink waiting for me. I knew that was her attempt to get some quality time and dick. But after keeping up with the twins' crying, feedings, and diaper changes, we talked until obviously falling asleep. I had convinced her that I would think about being a real family, figuring that would buy her silence until I found the courage to tell her the truth. I hoped that if she knew that I had a woman, she would be cool and maybe I wouldn't have to tell Jada so soon.

"I was supposed to meet up with King." Then I looked at my phone and lied again. "Shit, he been callin' me too." But it wasn't King that had been blowing my phone up. It was Jada.

"Okay. Are you coming back?"

I quickly told her, "I'll let you know," as I rushed toward the door and let myself out, not giving her the chance to further question me. I got out of that building so fast that you would've thought that the police were chasing me out of that motherfucker. I jumped in my ride and sped through the city, running lights, and up the expressway, dipping lanes.

By the time that I pulled into my driveway, Jada hadn't called again, and I prayed to God that she was asleep. But I guess God wasn't issuing anymore ghetto blessings because as soon as I walked through the door, I was met by her burning, tear-soaked eyes.

"Where the fuck have you been?"

JADA

I didn't care if I woke up the kids. I was *pissed*. On top of everything that was falling apart around us, on top of our friends breaking bad on us, I didn't need my relationship falling apart and Dolla breaking bad on me too.

"I fell asleep," he said as he closed the door.

I was so hurt. Beyond the fact that he was obviously fucking with a bitch, he was digging the knife in deeper by disrespecting me with lies that weren't even believable.

"Nigga, I've been with you since I was a kid! I know when the fuck you lyin'! You went to take care of business, so where were you taking care of business at that was comfortable enough for you to fall the fuck to sleep?"

He tried to buy time to think of another lie by saying, "You need to calm down. You gon' wake up the kids."

"I don't give a fuck!" I shouted.

He rushed toward me, saying, "Jada, baby, c'mon—"

He reached out to grab me, but I smacked his arms away. "Don't fucking touch me! I know you're fucking around on me again, Dolla! The phone calls! You're hidin' your phone and shit!"

"Baby, I swear—"

"Don't lie! Stop fucking lyin'! I'm not crazy!" As I plopped down on the couch with tears streaming down my face, I was sure that I looked absolutely crazy. However, as crazy as I may have seemed, I knew I was right.

When he sat close beside me, I scooted away from him like he was a stranger. But a stranger to his bullshit, I was not. I knew him like the back of my hand. I had been catching this nigga up in random pussy since we were kids, and at twenty-five, I was so done with it. But this...this was *different*. I couldn't believe that, with all of the shit we were facing with Siren and Meech, Dolla would even have his mind on pussy right now. That made me feel like the bitch was of some importance or they had a deep connection. And that shit broke my heart.

"Are you cheating on me, Dolla?" I couldn't even look him in the eyes. Mine were shut tight, fighting the oncoming of a mental breakdown due to all the important things that were falling apart around me. "Just tell me now, because if I—"

"I'm not cheating on you, ba—"

"Don't lie—"

"I'm not lying!"

My eyes shot open, and when I looked into his, I saw nothing but lies.

I jumped to my feet, full of regret and disappointment, and marched toward the stairs. "Fuck you, Dolla. I hope she's worth it."

MEECH

I had been hanging out with London every day. I was feeling her, but I was honestly using her. Being around her helped me forget about the bullshit that I was facing in my crew, and in my home. But I liked her so much that I hadn't fucked her yet. I wanted to make sure that she was real, because after the stunt Siren had pulled, I didn't trust my own judgment. I felt myself falling for shorty, but I needed to pace myself and make sure that she was genuine before I gave another chick my heart.

She hadn't been pressing me for dick either. I assumed that she was doing the same; taking it slow and feeling me out. So when she invited me over to her crib Sunday afternoon, I thought nothing of it. Yet, I did think it was strange when she texted the invitation from a different number.

Meech: *Why are you texting me from another phone?*

London: *This is my mom's phone. We'll talk about it when you get here.*

Here we go, was all I thought as I made my way to her crib. Although I was feeling her, I had only known her for a short while and I figured her ratchedness, which we all have, would fall out of the closet soon enough. This shit felt like drama, and a nigga like me had no room for another dramatic chick.

I prepared myself for the bullshit as I rang the doorbell, but I wasn't at all prepared for what I saw when she opened the door.

"What the fuck happened to you?"

She shied away from my stare in embarrassment. She bowed her head in shame and walked away from the door, leaving me to enter and lock it on my own.

I didn't mean to be so insensitive, but seeing her like that threw me off. Just last night, she was flawless, but between then and now, someone had fucked her face up. Her face was black and blue, and there was a huge bandage across her cheek.

"What happened, ma?" I asked again as I followed her toward the couch.

"I got mugged."

"Mugged?"

She plopped down on the couch with her lip poked out. I sat beside her, in awe of how beautiful she still looked with a black eye.

"Yeah. I was leaving out for work when this chick just came outta nowhere and rushed me. She punched me in the eye, and then the nose. She tried to take my purse. When I wouldn't let go, she sliced me across the face with a razor and took my phone and my purse."

"You don't know who it was?"

"No," she whined. "But ain't no tellin' in this neighborhood. She was probably some thirsty-ass bitch trying to come up on a quick lick because she didn't get her link card this month. She's lucky she caught me off guard, otherwise I would've fucked her up." Then she sighed dramatically. "I fucking hate living over here. I can't wait to move."

"Then why don't you?"

"You know I just moved to Chicago a few months ago. I just got a job a few weeks ago, so I gotta save to move. But as soon as I do, I'm outta here."

Just then, I shocked myself. I had an urge to tell her that I would get her a place anywhere she wanted, but I mentally grabbed that thought and put it in a chokehold.

But getting her a phone would be okay. "C'mon," I said as I stood and took her by the hand.

"Where are we going?"

"To get you a new phone."

"No, Meech. You don't have to do that."

"Yes, I do. How else am I going to talk to you?" I asked with a flirtatious grin.

She smiled. "I'm not going outside with this black eye."

I shrugged. "You still look pretty."

Her shoulders relaxed as she stared up at me, seemingly in awe of my ability to make her feel good in this moment.

I grabbed her chin, bent down and kissed her slowly but aggressively, trying to take her pain and worry away with my tongue. My dick did cartwheels inside of my Robbins jeans. I wanted in that pussy so bad, but I had to think with my head and not my dick.

"C'mon," I said, grabbing her hand again and pulling her up. Now she was too weak from my aggression to fight me. "You can just tell everybody I did it."

We broke out into laughs as she reluctantly followed me. It was then, in that moment, that I knew that shorty was going to be in my life for a long time. I just didn't know how.

****

After taking London to Sprint to get her phone, we got some takeout and hung out at her crib. Back at her house, she removed the bandage and showed me the cut across her face.

It wasn't deep enough that it needed stitches, so luckily, it would heal without much scarring.

Laying up with her as we watched Netflix movies put even more pressure on me to figure out how to get rid of Siren. The urgency wasn't to replace her with London. Although I liked London, I barely knew her to the capacity that I was ready to wife her. But as I lay with her in her mama's house, she fussed about not being able to even afford her own place or a new phone. I thought it was so unfair for that lying-ass bitch, Siren, to be riding around in foreign cars wearing designer shoes and purses, all of which *I* had funded, while this genuine girl was struggling. True, there could be some deceit and shadiness in London's personality. I didn't know her well enough to think otherwise. But she had shown me more love in the few days that I'd known her than the motherfuckas I'd known for years.

As we laid in her bed, I asked her, "Why you ain't got no man?"

It was a cliché-ass question. But she was obviously beautiful. She was a dream for a man with a fetish for curves, thick thighs, and a phat ol' ass. But she also seemed to be a sweet, easy-going, and down to earth girl. I couldn't imagine her door being free of niggas beating it down, but as I had spent these days with her, her phone rarely rang, and she wasn't sneakily reading and sending text messages.

"Well," she said with a sigh. "I've been taking a break. My last relationship was a motherfucka. My ex was an asshole that kicked me out so that his new bitch could move in—"

"Damn."

"I know, right? That's how I ended up moving back to Chicago and in with my mama. Me and his side bitch fought for two years before she finally won, if you can call being with him *winning*. So I've just been enjoying being single and drama free. I haven't been dating because every nigga I meet seems be on some bullshit. I'm sick of niggas with wives, lying and playing games."

I swallowed the large, guilty lump in my throat as I asked, "So why are you dating me?"

She lifted her head from my chest and looked at me with a questioning smirk. "We're *dating*?"

"Not right this minute because you don't wanna go nowhere with that black-ass eye."

Her mouth dropped and she hit my chest playfully as she laughed at my joke. When she laid her head back down on my chest, I had to check myself, because the feeling of her laying on me felt too good.

KENNEDY

I couldn't believe that I was actually having dinner with my dad. It had been so long since we had spent this kind of quality time together. It hadn't happened since I was eighteen. Although we had reconciled and he had attended my wedding, I was even more convinced that I had my daddy back in my life as I sat at his kitchen table. I watched him hovering over the frying pan at the stove. The sight reminded me of the single father who had raised me so lovingly and took such good care of me, even though he was strict as all hell.

I was relieved to be at his place. Being there was like an escape from reality, or a mini vacation. Not that my reality was all that bad, but my mind was racing when I was at home. I couldn't help but feel like Jada and Siren were lying when they said nothing was going on. I could feel the tension while in Cabo and even at Brooklyn's birthday party. They are all acting funny and keeping me out of the loop like I was still a little ass kid. But I was thinking that maybe it was best that I didn't know what was going on. I had spent three years in turmoil. These past days of freedom had been the best I'd felt in years, and I wasn't ready to come down off my cloud just yet.

Whatever it was, they could continue to keep me out of it.

"Guess what, Dad?"

He quickly shot a curious look at me over his shoulder before he returned his attention to the frying pan. "What?"

"I'm going to start school in the fall."

"Really?" he asked with excitement in his tone.

"Yep. I re-enrolled the other day."

"That's awesome! You're still going to study psychiatry?"

"Yep. King said that he's going to help me start my own practice once I am done with my degrees and licensing."

"Speaking of King, how was the honeymoon?"

I smiled behind his back as I thought of the great sex that King and I had in that villa, on the sand, in the Jacuzzi, and everywhere else we felt like it on the island. "It was great."

"The wedding was quite a production. That man must really love you."

Again, I smiled. "He does."

Then, my dad reduced the fire under the frying pan and sat across from me. "I hate to admit this, but being at that wedding and watching you two made me see the love and loyalty between you and him. I began to understand why you served that time for him."

Instantly, the tears started. At that table, I was no longer King's woman. I was the little girl that had always wanted nothing but her father's approval. And finally, after so long, I'd gotten it.

"I'm so sorry, Daddy," I cried. "I know that I let you down."

He reached over and took my hand into his. "No, *I'm* the one who's sorry."

I looked at him curiously. "Why?"

"Because I wasn't there for you when you needed me. I should've been there during your sentencing. I know that I couldn't have served that time with you, but I can't imagine you being in that place alone and I wouldn't even answer the phone." Tears were now coming to his eyes as he said, "I'm so sorry that I wasn't there for you. I am *so sorry*."

I smiled into his eyes. "It's okay, Daddy. I wasn't alone. I had someone to take care of me."

CHAPTER TWELVE

KENNEDY

February 14, 2013

"Happy Valentine's Day, baby."

I sucked my teeth and frowned as I admired King from across the table where we sat in the visitation room. "Yeah right."

King reached across the table and gently squeezed my hand. He couldn't do much more. We were only allowed minimal physical contact at the start and end of each visit. Long or passionate embraces or kisses were not permitted, and could have resulted in a visit being terminated.

"You're so beautiful," he told me.

I sucked my teeth again and rolled my eyes back to the furthest part of my head. He was just being nice. My hair was so dry from the bullshit shampoo that they had in here that my ponytail was frizzy and brittle. The jumpsuit that I was wearing was a bit too big. I had started to lose weight because, besides the fact that I hated the food, the anxiety of missing my King and Kayla every day left me with little to no appetite anyway. Ms. Jerry had helped me get a hold of some foundation, but I wasn't using it to look pretty. My skin had surprisingly cleared up so well during my incarceration. But my nails weren't even done. Although it sounded superficial as hell, being locked up in this place made a girl miss and appreciate the smallest things like flat irons, and a gel overlay. Making it worse was King sitting across from me in Givenchy jeans, a Dolce & Gabbana leather jacket, Gucci boots, and jewels that I was slobbering over. He was every girl's dope boy dream as he sat across from me with that kissable face and his dreads tied at the top of his head.

King couldn't even argue with my attitude. He looked at me as if there was so much that he wanted to say, but he just stared at me sympathetically.

The way that we watched one another was so pathetic. I wanted to be happy to see him. But the sadness in the realization that I would not be able to walk out of this motherfucker with him outweighed any smile that I wanted to give him.

"Anyway," I sighed. "How is Kayla?"

"She's great." And this I knew, because besides monthly visits, he made sure to answer my call every day. "I got some pictures to show you."

It was so sad to see King in this place. Every time he visited me, he was the total opposite of his usual self. He was sad, he was weak, and he was fragile. It was heartbreaking to watch.

I watched King as he reached into his pocket and took out some photos. Cell phones weren't allowed inside of visits, so each time King visited, he printed out pictures to show me.

I leaned as he showed me so many pictures of Kayla, who was now ten months old. He told me how she was now standing up on her own against tables and chairs. Her smile was so contagious that as I looked at the pictures, the bubbly personality of her smile had taken over mine, causing me to smile brightly. Her hair had grown so long since the last pictures that I'd seen. It was so dark, curly and shiny in its ponytails.

But as I wondered who had dressed her in each lacy, fluffy, adorable outfit and who'd put her hair in each ponytail and tied every ribbon, my heart broke because it wasn't me.

Whomever had dressed her so lovingly, wasn't her mother.

As I sat back away from the pictures, and welcomed the tears that were preparing to marathon their way down my cheeks, King gave me the same sympathetic look that he always gave me during his visits. But we ignored the elephant in the room, not wanting to fill the little time that we had together with regrets and disappointments.

At the end of the visit, we said our goodbyes with a hug and kiss that couldn't last that long.

He whispered, "I love you, baby," as I let him go.

I promised him, "I love you too...so much. Happy Valentine's Day."

We didn't let go of one another's hands until he had walked so far way that he could no longer hold the tips of my fingers.

As the guard walked me and the other prisoners back to our cells, I fought the urge to cry. I fought the urge to break down in front of these bitches. I fought the desire to run after King, pass the guards, and get far the fuck away from this place.

As I walked back into my cell, both Dre and Ms. Jerry looked at me with wide eyes full of wonder, though Ms. Jerry's were obviously so tired. Today, her blood pressure was high and her feet, legs, and ankles were swollen due to the lupus.

"Did he notice?" Dre asked frantically.

I sighed as I plopped down on the bed between them, saying, "No."

"See?" Ms. Jerry asked. "I told you that you couldn't see it."

Subconsciously, I reached up and touched my eye. Underneath the foundation was shades of black and blue. I had gotten jumped on the yard a few days prior by bitches who knew me from Chicago. They were some hood bitches who wanted to be with King, but never had a chance. They hated me for being Mrs. Carter. Stupid bitches didn't realize that although I was his wife, I was in this motherfucker with them, so technically, I didn't have him either. They didn't care either way. They talked shit to me every day, but I had already been told that if I stayed out of trouble, I could get out a year early on good behavior. No matter how much I wanted to stomp a hole in these ugly, petty, simple-ass bitches, reuniting with my man and daughter was much more important, so I ignored them. Then, a few days ago, I guess they'd had enough of seeing me breathe, so they jumped me. I was handling those two bitches, but not like I would have if it had been a one-on-one fight. However, I got help from Dre, who ripped the second bitch off of me and beat her until she was unconscious.

I couldn't let King see my eye. He couldn't know that I was in here in any kind of danger because it would make the rest of my time in here unbearable for him. It was unbearable enough for me, and Kayla didn't need two broken parents.

And there I was, as always, looking out for King way more than I was looking out for myself.

Chapter Thirteen

KING

"Yes, King!" she breathed. "Oh, *God*, yes!"

"Grrr," was all that I could manage to growl as I fought the urge to cum right then.

Kennedy swore that she never masturbated while she was locked up, and I believed her. This motherfucker was tight as air, and as I hit it doggy-style in the middle of our California king at seven in the morning, I fought the urge to cum when I had just really gotten in the pussy.

"Fuck," I groaned as I smacked her ass. "I missed this pussy, girl."

When she shot back, "I missed this dick, Daddy," I damn near lost my mind. I held on to her waist so that I could control the steadiness of my strokes while fighting the sensation to burst inside of her.

"Gawd damn, this pussy's so *fuckin'* wet, baby," I serenaded her, and all she gave me back were moans and deep breaths.

I was going to cum. I knew it. To prevent it, I pulled out, turned Kennedy over on her back, and then dove face first into the pussy.

"Shit!" she breathed as I sucked her clit.

I sucked it slowly while my tongue flicked it hard and fast. My finger went into her leaking pussy. I found her G-spot and pressed it repeatedly.

"Oh my God!"

I spit her clit out of my mouth only long enough to order, "Cum for me, baby."

She tried to fight against me. She tried to run away, but with one of my massive, dark chocolate, muscular arms wrapped around her thigh, keeping the pussy right where I wanted it with no mercy, she wasn't going anywhere.

"Fuck!" she squealed as I returned to sucking the cum out of her.

To persuade her orgasm, I left her clit briefly, took my tongue and licked from my finger, which was still inside of her, back up to her clit. Then I spit and slurped it up into a suction that she couldn't fight.

"*Shiiit!*"

"That's it, baby," I encouraged her with a mouth full of pussy. "C'mon. Cum for me."

And that's just what she did. She came all over my finger and in my mouth, and my baby, my *Reina*, tasted so good.

I left my meal and laid over her missionary style, slipping my dick into its tight home before she even had the opportunity to recover from her orgasm. Both of us were silenced by orgasms that were building between us. We could only breathe heavily as the sensation built between us.

"Can I cum in you, baby?"

She looked at me like I was crazy. Since getting out of prison, she had been making me pull out because her appointment to get on birth control wasn't until June. But for all I cared, she didn't have to get on that shit. My baby could have as many babies as she wanted as far as I was concerned.

"Please, baby? I want my baby boy."

Never the one to be able to tell me no, she just hesitated. But I was always the one to make sure she got exactly what she wanted. So, just as I felt myself cumming, I pulled out and told her, "Come catch it, baby."

She jumped onto her knees and caught my nut just in time for me to shoot it down her throat while she sucked me dry.

"Aaaggghhh!" I was barely able to keep my balance. I buckled, the great sensation making me weak. I balanced myself on her back with one hand while she continued to suck me dry.

"Shit!" I cursed through a growl. "Fuck! Okay, baby. Okay!"

As I pushed her back and fell on my back onto the bed, she giggled.

"Ain't nothin' funny," I breathed as I pulled her down on top of me.

The sweat on our skin mixed with one another's as she lay on my chest.

I kissed her on top of the head as I asked her, "Why you won't give me my boy?"

She sighed heavily. "King..."

"You're not ready for another baby?"

"You don't want another baby. You want a *boy*. What if it's not a boy? I gotta have another baby in order to keep trying?"

"I'll take a boy or girl, honestly."

"But you really want a boy."

I chuckled. "I do."

She traced my chest with her fingertips as she said, "I just got out, King. I'm not ready to have another baby yet. There are so many things that I want to do that I haven't been able to. I know that you'll take care of me and our kids, and make sure that I will have all the help I need, but I really want to focus on being Kennedy right now and fulfilling my dreams."

Again, I kissed her on the top of her head. "I understand, baby."

"Plus, Kayla's ass barely likes me. I can't take two kids with funky-ass attitudes."

We broke out into laughs as I wrapped my arms around her and held her tight. "Kayla loves you, and I do too."

MEECH

The next day, I chose to give London some space. I felt like using her to avoid the shit going on around me wasn't fair. But, surprisingly, as I stood to leave the back office of the convenience store, I couldn't believe that I missed her.

"Shit, nigga." I was caught by surprise when I was leaving out of the door and nearly collided with Brooklyn. "You scared the fuck outta me. What's up?"

"What up, cuz?"

We shook up as we met in the doorway. This convenience store was one of the many front businesses we owned to clean our money, but this was the main spot where we kept an enormous amount of cash, and a money counter in the backroom that served as an office for many members of our organization.

"What's going on, man? How did things go while we were gone? No problems, right?" I asked him.

I knew that he was in charge while we were away in Cabo, but truth be told, I had really distanced myself from everybody, so I didn't have much of a clue as to what was going on.

"Everything went smooth. I even chopped it up with this new buyer."

My eyebrow instantly curled. "Word? You ran that by King?"

"Yeah. I spoke to him about it while he was in Cabo. He didn't tell you?"

I didn't want to tell Brooklyn that I had spent the whole damn trip avoiding King and Siren, so I just asked, "Who is this new buyer?"

King, Dolla and I didn't do shit like this. We had main buyers that we had developed trusting relationships with over the years. Who they distributed to was their business, but the waiting list was long for buyers who wanted to purchase directly from us because we had the highest quality product with the best prices, thanks to Gustavo. We had been working with him for so many years that he was giving us his high quantity product at ridiculous wholesale prices. We liked that working relationship and wanted to keep his trust by not fucking with the wrong people and drawing the wrong attention.

"One of my boys who deals introduced me to him. He's from the west coast and looking to cop before he goes back to the crib."

"What's his name?"

"Black."

I shrugged. "Never heard of him."

"He's all good. I spoke to him a few times to feel him out. I told him that I got *that work*, so he ready."

Again, I wondered why King would be cool with this shit, but figured that if he was talking to Brooklyn while he was in Cabo, King wasn't focused, nor was he probably even sober. But the buyer was copping from *Brooklyn* and not us, so the shit was on him if this nigga, Black, was shady.

"What's been up with you?" Brooklyn asked. "Ain't heard from you in a minute. You even missed my party, man."

"I just been chillin'," I simply told him.

He gave me a suspicious look and just stood there silent.

"What, nigga?" I asked with a chuckle.

"Something's up with you. You seem off."

"Off?"

"Yeah. Like you off your square."

I laughed to throw him off because I respected the man too much to lie to his face. Although he had just moved here two years ago, and was my second cousin, we had become pretty tight. I had promised his mother that I would look out for him while he was here, so I had been keeping him under my wing until shit hit the fan a few days ago. So, of course, he would notice my sudden distance.

"C'mon, bruh. Holla at me," he insisted as he leaned against the wall.

I shrugged slightly as I put my hands in my pockets. "I'm just not feeling a lot of shit that's going on. I'm questioning the loyalty of certain motherfuckers around me."

He raised his eyebrow high and asked, "Word?"

"Word," I answered with a nod. "But I ain't gon' get too deep into it. Trust me, if it's that deep, I'll be hollerin' at you."

As I reached out to shake up with him, he said, "That's what's up."

"I'm outta here, though."

"Later, cuz."

JADA

"You think I need to put up with this shit, Dolla? I'm only twenty-five years old. All I got is two kids. I can get out here and get a nigga that won't cheat on me! I don't have to deal with this shit."

Dolla gave me a menacing look as he reached the stop sign. "Don't say no shit like that to me ever again."

As we glared at one another, I hated him for being so fucking cute. Those pretty eyes, heavy lids giving him a constant sultry look, and pretty boy face wrapped in smooth chocolate on a six-foot two, slim, muscular frame were the exact reasons why these bitches were willing to fuck him behind my back.

I sucked my teeth and looked out of the window. "Fuck you, Dolla."

"What are you dealing with?" he fussed. "Is it a bitch calling your phone claiming me? Is it some bitch on Facebook in a picture with me? On Instagram? Or any of that other social media shit y'all be on? No, it's not!"

"But I still know she exists! I'm not stupid, Dolla!"

I was still pissed from last night. I knew this nigga was on bullshit. It was eating me up so bad that I couldn't even sleep the night before. I remembered how hurt I was when he had pulled this shit a few years ago. When I would argue with him about bitch after bitch, he would have the nerve to slap me when I wouldn't stop questioning him. We had grown, I thought. We were a much tighter knit family and we had matured into two people who would ride or die like a motherfucker for each other. Therefore, I couldn't believe that he would break that bond by slipping back into his old, deceitful, sneaky ways.

"Jada," he called my name softly, but I didn't respond. I just stared out of the window wondering how the fuck my life got here. Three weeks ago, I was happy. I was content with my life, my friends, and my family. Now it all could potentially be taken away from me because the motherfuckers that I had chosen to love weren't shit!

"I love you," I heard him say. "I'm not sleeping with nobody else, I promise."

I sighed deeply, hoping he would shut the fuck up. I didn't want to hear his voice. Shit, I didn't even want to be near him, but I'd agreed to ride with him to Meech's crib. He wanted to see where Meech and Siren's heads were at. So he told Meech that we were coming over to hang out, which usually meant he and Meech would get drunk in the den while me and Siren would get wasted upstairs.

That's exactly what happened too. As soon as we got to Meech's house, he opened the door with a drink already in hand.

He gave us a dry, "What up?"

That feeling of some shady shit happening deepened in my spirit. I had never seen Meech so distant, so cold. Siren being on bullshit wouldn't make his attitude *this* fucked up. It was something more, and I knew it.

He and Dolla shook up as we made our way into the home.

Meech told me, "Siren is upstairs," as he and Dolla headed toward the den.

I reluctantly went up the stairs. I was too stressed out about everything. I just wanted to be home in my own bed, not trying to feel out this shady-ass bitch.

Automatically, I went into their bedroom but remembered that Meech had kicked that ass out, so with a chuckle, I made my way to the guest room where I heard the television on.

Siren was lying across the bed, comfortably watching TV, and I was disgusted that she could be so relaxed in her deceit. For years, this bitch had walked around like she was a true friend, but she was the person that King had torn the city apart looking for, hoping to find whoever was responsible for his girl being behind bars. He wanted to put the motherfucker six feet deep. The shit was fucked up, and it showed all over my face as I walked into the room and sat in a chair against the wall across from the bed.

"What's up?" she asked me as she turned the television's volume down.

"Shit," I answered. "Dolla came over to hang out with Meech for a minute."

She chuckled and shook her head at me. "You got a lot of nerve, Jada."

I frowned. "Why you say that?"

"You sitting there with that attitude like you didn't shoot me, bitch." When she giggled, it was further confirmation that this hoe was crazy as fuck. She wasn't even mad that I'd popped her! But that let me know that she was truly on bullshit. She obviously wasn't mad about it because deep down inside, she didn't blame me. She knew she deserved it.

"C'mon, Jada," she whined as she sat on the bed. "I miss my friend."

Truth be told, I missed my bestie too. But this chick sitting on the bed wasn't the girl that I had been friends with since I was a kid. I didn't know who *this bitch* was.

She folded her arms across her chest and shook her head again. "I can't believe that you really think that I was the one snitching."

"I saw you with the detective!"

"And I told you why!"

"Even if you didn't say anything this time, you're the reason why Kennedy went to prison. What if King had been in that car? What if Dolla or Meech had been driving? You didn't give a fuck about whose life you were about to ruin that night."

"I thought *King* would be driving," she said as if that was a good defense.

I asked her sarcastically, "And that's better?"

"You don't know what you would've done in that situation, Jada. And you better pray to God that you never are. Just like Kennedy chose to save her family and take that charge, I chose to save mine too. I feel like shit for what I did and I feel bad about it every day—"

"So what? You expect me to just forgive you for putting my cousin in prison, for snitching on my people?"

"I was your people *first.*"

"Exactly. We were like sisters, and you didn't think about what would happen to me or how I would feel when you tried to take from me. By sending my cousin to prison, you took from me and my family! We were hurt over that shit. You thought King would be in the car. That's taking from me too because without him, the money would have stopped, and my family wouldn't have been eating."

I ran my hand through my weave in frustration. This was all too overwhelming. My heart was beating at an uncontrollable rate, and my fucking head was spinning. I was beyond done with her and Dolla. I wanted away from both of their asses.

"Meech got him a new girl."

I looked at Siren like she had lost her mind. Clearly, she had. She had said that shit like I gave a fuck or as if I wanted to sit and have girl talk with her shady ass.

Bitch, we are not, friends, I thought as I just stared at her.

"I thought you were going to talk to him for me."

"You in the house, ain't you?" I shot.

"But he's not with me. He got me sleeping in a whole other room while he's fucking with some bitch." Then a sinister grin spread across her face as she said, "I whooped that bitch's ass, though."

My judgmental expression deepened. "You did what?"

"Yep," she smiled with a nod of the head. "I sure did. I snuck up on her. I didn't want her to know who I was because I can't have Meech even madder at me. But I followed them last night to the Loca Lounge. Then I sat out there 'til they left. They went to this house around the spot on the south side. I went back the next morning and waited for her to come outside. I dragged that ass and sliced her face up. Then I took the bitch's phone, since she wanna use it to call my man."

I simply said, "You are crazy as hell," as I stood to leave.

Although she was crazy, I couldn't blame her for this particular crazy stunt because I felt like finding whoever the bitch was that Dolla was fucking with, and dragging that ass too.

"You leavin'?" Siren asked me.

"Hell yeah," I answered as I walked toward the door

I didn't even say anything else. I just walked out. But as I descended the stairs, I saw that she had returned to lying across the bed comfortably like nothing was wrong.

These motherfuckers were draining me. Her and Dolla. I couldn't take breathing the same air as them anymore. I was about to take a fucking Uber home.

Chapter Fourteen

KENNEDY

I was so happy that my cell phone was ringing. I had been browsing Instagram while watching a marathon of Snapped and enjoying the quiet house, since Kayla was in daycare. Now that I had been home for some time, King and I let her go back to daycare. The nanny only came when we needed her because I no longer wanted somebody else raising my daughter.

I was bored as all hell, though. Sitting in the house every day may sound enjoyable to some, but I was already bored to death. There was only so much shopping and going out to eat that a girl could do. I was actually thinking about asking King if I could start my own business. I was thinking of opening a cute boutique like the ones I followed on Instagram. I was definitely looking forward to starting school in the fall, and I figured both school and a side business of my own would keep me very busy.

When I recognized the in-coming phone number that was calling my cell, I eagerly picked up and answered.

"Hello. This is a pre-paid debit call from...Dre...an inmate at the Logan Correctional Facility." I instantly started grinning. "To accept this call, please press zero now. To—"

I quickly pressed zero to accept the call and turned down the television in the bedroom as I shouted, "Dre!"

"Don't Dre me! I'm mad at you."

"I know. You didn't have to curse me out in your letter either." As we spoke, I could hear the rowdiness of the inmates around her who were on the phone as well.

"I just ain't understand why it was takin' you so long to hit me with your info," Dre fussed.

"It's been a lot going on since the moment I got out."

"I know. I heard about that bomb-ass wedding."

"How did you hear about it?"

"My sister was telling me about it when I called home yesterday. She said y'all's hashtag was trending on Instagram and shit."

I smiled, the romantic residue of the wedding still running rampant through my spirit. "Yeah, it was pretty dope. Actually, it was better than dope."

"That's what's up. Hate I couldn't be there."

"How are you doing in there?" I asked Dre.

"I'm good...hangin' on."

"How is Ms. Jerry?"

When she paused briefly, I knew she was about to lie.

She finally answered, "S-she...she's good."

"Don't lie to me, Dre."

"I'm not."

"You stuttered."

"You shouldn't be worried about shit that's going on in here. Your mind should be far away from this place."

"I know, but you know I'm worried about her." I paused, waiting on Dre to say something, *anything*, but she wouldn't. So I just sighed and said, "Just tell her to call me when she feels up to it." However, I made a mental note to call Ms. Jerry's son, who I'd gotten to know during calls during my incarceration when Ms. Jerry had been too weak to call him herself.

"Bet."

As Dre started telling me about things that had been going on since I'd left, I lay back with a smile on my face. It was crazy how, although I'd hated being in prison, I missed so many people there, especially Ms. Jerry and Dre. But I would prefer missing them to being in there with them any day.

DOLLA

I gotta do something, I thought as I stared at Meagan's judgmental eyes. *I can't keep doing this shit.*

"C'mooon," she begged in a feminine moan that made my dick hard. "The kids are asleep. I haven't been fucked in forever."

"And you can't until after you get your checkup. You can't wait a few days?"

She stomped her foot lightly on the carpet. "Fine. Let me give you some head then."

I chuckled so hard that my head fell back against the couch. "You're crazy, girl."

"I'm serious, Dolla. I'm horny as fuck."

My eyebrow rose slightly. "And sucking my dick would cure that?"

The way that she licked her lips, and stared at me seductively with those caramel eyes when she said, "Yes," made my dick instantly jump.

She took my silence as consent and walked toward me slowly. Everything in my mind was against this shit. I should've been sitting here telling her the truth, not getting my dick sucked. I didn't want to make her heartbreak worse when she found out the truth by giving her false hope with dick. But as she dropped down to her knees in front of me, and that plump booty spread out into a heart before me, my dick started taking over all of my common sense. She continued staring at me with those sultry eyes until I was now looking at the top of her big, curly hair. As she reached into my basketball shorts and pulled my dick out, it hardened against her French manicured fingertips.

"Ssssss..." I hated the way that I reacted so suddenly to the feeling of her warm mouth around my dick. Since Jada had her suspicions about this very thing, she hadn't fucked me since we got back from Cabo, so this head felt *great*.

But as I sat there with my head back and my hand in Meagan's curls, I kept saying to myself, *I have to tell her.*

I had to and *soon.* I had enough outside drama as is with Meech acting like he was gon' get ghost on us in any minute. There was already stress in my business. I didn't need my home life fucked up too. The only way to make things halfway right with Jada was to be honest with Meagan. Meagan was much more understanding than Jada because she had a lot less invested in me. I would rather tell her the truth so that she would understand my unavailability. That way, she would stop wondering why I wasn't with her, and I could stop sneaking over here every other day, which would then please

Jada. That way, I would have a little less stress until I figured out when to break this news to Jada.

Yeah, I'll just tell her the truth, I thought as my dick hit the back of her throat repeatedly. *Not tonight, though. Right now, I'm 'bout to get this nut.*

MEECH

♪I know you got all dressed up for the club
Waiting on a nigga to come pick you up
Baby, when I saw ya walking out the door
I just knew ya needed something more

Now whip it straight back to the crib
Finna give you something that you won't forget

Baby, I just wanna get you out them clothes
I just wanna see you dance in...

Slow motioooon♪

I couldn't believe this shit. Here I was sitting in my truck with London in front of her mother's house with Trey Songz flowing through the speakers while we kissed like we were teenagers. Shit, I hadn't done that since I was fifteen probably.

I couldn't help myself, though. On the one hand, I was feeling London. But on the other hand, I wondered if I was feeling her so much on some rebound shit. I wondered was I so fucked up over Siren's lie, that I was hopping on the next big ass and pretty smile just because it made me feel all better.

While out with her that day, something told me that that wasn't the case, though. Her eye had healed well enough that the bruises could be covered with makeup, so she let me take her to SLR Bar and Grill in Harvey for drinks and some food. As we had a bite to eat and plenty of drinks, I felt like my attraction to shorty was real, but it was new as hell to a nigga.

I had gotten with Siren because she was there. She was around, and I wanted what Dolla and King had. And that's not to denounce the significance of our relationship, because I did grow to have love for her. But it was the same kind of love that I felt for Dolla, Kennedy, and Jada, and the love I used to feel for King. Being with London made me wonder how my love for Siren had turned to hate so quickly. Was the shit really unconditional love to begin with? Unconditional love is what you need to really fuck with someone for life. Obviously King had been shady with Kennedy from jump, but *Kennedy*? She loved King unconditionally. Whatever move he made, she was right there, riding with loyalty and *trust*. She didn't love that nigga out of obligation or because of what he could do for her. She sincerely loved him *unconditionally*. I loved Elijah unconditionally. He could do whatever, and I would never lose that love for him. He wasn't even my biological son, but I loved that lil' boy. His mama had done the unthinkable, but she was still in my house because of how I felt for *him,* not her.

That was unconditional love. But as for Siren and the love I once had for her, that shit was gone that fast. Dead. Adios.

So, I wondered had it been real love to begin with. Or had a nigga just been coasting for all these years?

"What's wrong with you?"

I opened my eyes when I heard her voice, not even realizing that she had stopped kissing me. "Huh?"

"What's wrong?"

I swallowed hard, attempting to swallow all of my reality so that I could just chill with this pretty-ass girl and stay in the moment.

"Nothing," I answered.

Then I grabbed the back of her head, clutched a hand full of her locs, brought her face to mine and sucked those juicy-ass lips.

"Mmm," she moaned into my mouth. "Shit, Meech. I want to give you this pussy so bad."

Well damn.

I instantly stopped kissing her and stared into her eyes, saying nothing. I felt conflicted. I wanted that pussy. For many reasons, I hadn't taken it. Plus, I knew shorty had drank enough to alter her reasonable judgment.

"Please take it," she begged. "I appreciate you being a gentleman, but I really want to give you this pussy. Just take it." When she saw me still hesitating, she added another, "Please?"

Fuck.

What she didn't realize was that I wasn't being a gentleman in that sense. I wasn't trying to show her that I wanted more than sex from her, in the way that it may have seemed. I was just trying to keep shorty out of my drama.

However, considering the way that she was rubbing my thigh with that sensual look in her eyes and that pouty-ass mouth, I was willing to risk it at the moment.

"Please?" she insisted.

Fine. Fuck it, I said to myself.

When I turned the engine off, she stopped me, "No. Not in my mama's house. She's home. Let's go to your house."

Gawd damn it. I started to freak out. *Think quick. Think quick, nigga.*

"We can't," I said with a look full of disappointment. "My cousin is there babysitting Elijah and considering the way I'm about to fuck you, you won't be able to keep quiet."

My aggression overtook her, causing her eyes to ride heavy with lust as she bit her bottom lip and suggested, "Let's go get a room then."

****

On the way to the hotel, I stopped and got some drinks and condoms. Then I booked the Luxe room, a penthouse with two floors and steam spa shower for two with three rain showerheads, at Aura Suites.

"Damn," London fussed as she sucked her teeth and stood over the wet bar. "We need ice."

"I got it. Hand me the ice bucket."

Although we'd had plenty of drinks at dinner, I needed more. I knew what I wanted. I wanted far, deep into that pussy, but in order to force back the darkness of my reality, I needed to be just a lil' bit tipsier.

When she handed me the bucket, I quickly jogged down the stairs of the suite and out of the door. I was so busy anticipating that light-skinned pussy that I didn't realize that somebody was approaching me.

"Really, nigga?"

I didn't even think. As soon as I saw Siren's face, the lust went away and anger took over. She was rushing toward me with rage and the same was for me. As soon as I was in arm's reach of her, I grabbed her shoulders, forced her a few feet away and pushed her against the brick wall of Room 123.

"The fuck is you doin'?"

My rage didn't scare her because her anger superseded mine, in her eyes. "No, what the fuck is *you* doin'?" she spat.

"Me! I'm doin' me, bitch!"

"I ain't gon' be too many more bitches!"

I had to laugh. Her audacity was so overwhelming that my anger went away and humor took over. I let her shoulders go, but she still stayed against the wall. The strap of her tank top had been ripped off of her shoulder due to my rage. She looked at me like she couldn't believe that I was laughing.

"You think this shit funny?" Her rage came out in short, deep breaths. "You at the hotel with a bitch? Really, nigga?"

She was actually genuinely hurt, and I believed it. In all of the years that we had been together, she had never caught me in this kind of position. I had been too loyal to her to allow that type of shit, but she'd taken that loyalty and showered it all on King.

"I can do what I wanna do. Last time I checked, you had lied to me for years and you weren't my girl no more."

She started to beg. "Meech—"

When I saw the longing in her eyes, I knew that even though she was obviously crazy as fuck, she wasn't so crazy that she wanted to fuck up the small chance with me that she thought she still had.

"If you still want a roof over your head, you'll leave right now," I told her.

"Nigga, I already told you if you kick me out, I'm taking Elijah with me."

I shrugged as if I didn't give two fucks. "Take him then."

I was full of shit. It would crush me if she took my son from me. He wasn't my biological son, but he was the closest thing that I had to a child, and I was the only father he knew.

But she believed my false bravery. Her anger simmered and was replaced with retreat.

She simply said, "Fuck you, Meech," as she stumped away.

I sighed heavily, gave up on the ice, and headed back to the room. I waited until I saw Siren's Porsche leave the parking lot before I went inside.

I gotta get rid of that bitch, I thought.

I had to. She was becoming too sporadic. I would never feel the same way about Siren again, but like Jada said, Siren knew too much. She knew codes, locations, and stash spots. Considering how angry, possessed, and crazy she was acting, she could send the cops or someone to any or all of our doorsteps to jack us. But I didn't know how much longer I could deal with her shit. I had to figure something out.

As I entered the suite, I realized that it was about time that I shared what was going on with the rest of the crew because I needed their help to get rid of Siren. Even if I wasn't fucking with King, I could at least holla at Dolla and Jada about it.

I climbed the staircase of the suite, ready to take my aggressions out on some pussy. London wanted this dick, and that's exactly what she was about to get.

But her snoring met me before I even entered the bedroom. She had passed out, red dreads everywhere as she lay fully clothed on her stomach.

Fuck!

CHAPTER FIFTEEN

KENNEDY

May 13, 2015

"You would get sick on my release day, wouldn't you?"

Ms. Jerry chuckled weakly as she lay on the bunk in her cell. "I'm alright."

She was lying. Every one of her limbs were swollen and each time she urinated, it was bloody, puffy, and bubbling, which were all signs that her kidneys were failing.

"Are you going to go see the doctor?" I asked her.

She nodded weakly. "As soon as I feel like getting up."

I sighed heavily and took in the sight of her one last time. "I love you, lady."

I really did. My mother had tried to be there for me as much as she could. She had answered every one of my phone calls and visited me every chance she could, but Ms. Jerry had been the consistent mother figure that I had needed for these past few years. Every night that I'd fought panic attacks, she had prayed for me. Every time that I was so sick because I missed my family to the point that I hadn't eaten in days, she prayed. Those days when I had to fight a bitch because she didn't like what my last name was, Dre had been right there, helping me whoop some ass. Then Ms. Jerry would clean our wounds and pray.

I loved her with all of my heart, and I also loved Dre, who was standing in the doorway of Ms. Jerry's cell waiting on me.

I bent over, kissed Ms. Jerry's cheek, and squeezed her swollen hand. "Bye," left my lips in cracks and then the tears came. "I love you."

"I love you too. You better send us your number right away so that we can call you."

Tears ran down my face as I promised, "I will."

She tapped my leg lightly, saying, "Stop crying and get on outta here. You got your man and baby waiting on you."

She was right, and I couldn't wait any longer to get to them, so I stood, taking her in one last time, and walked toward the door of the cell as tears streamed down my face. They were tears of sadness and joy, causing this moment to be way more overwhelming than I'd realized it would be.

"Make her go to the doctor," I told Dre.

The look on her face only made it even worse. She couldn't even look at me. She was still a female, but she hated identifying with one by being emotional or weak.

I saw her fighting tears and attempting to maintain strength as she spat, "I'll holla at you."

I smiled, saying, "You will." Then I stood on my tip toes to kiss her cheek. "Love you, Dre."

Her green eyes stared into mine. "I love you, too. Don't end up back in this motherfucka."

We both chuckled as I wrapped my arms around her. "I won't."

"A'ight, Carter. Time to go." At the sound of the guard's voice, I released Dre and gave her one last smile just as the guard took my arm to lead me away.

The walk through the prison to the visitation center again was mixed with sadness and joy. I never wanted to see this place again, but I was definitely leaving loved ones behind, and a piece of me as well.

But when the guard informed me that Miss Jada Davenport had checked in to pick me up and was waiting outside, my joy finally superseded my sadness. I couldn't get to that exit fast enough. As soon as I got there and the guard opened the door, the air hit me, and the realization that I was free overwhelmed me. I didn't know which car Jada had come to pick me up in, so as I descended the steps nervously, I fought to see through the windshields of the cars that were waiting for other inmates. My hands held my bag of so-called parting gifts tightly as I tried desperately to keep the weakness in my knees from causing me to fall down the concrete steps.

Then I heard a horn honk frantically as Jada's voice could be heard, shouting, "Someone play the horns and trumpets! Here comes the queen!"

I tried to hold back my smile. I tried to play it cool, as if I had done these past three years with ease. But when I saw Siren getting out of the backseat with my baby, and I heard Kayla's cries, I broke.

"Oh!" left my voice in a weep as tears flooded from my eyes yet again, and I took off running toward them.

I couldn't believe it. I was finally free. The past three years had been the most hurtful, darkest days of my life. But little did I know, as I ran into Jada and Siren's arms, that I would soon face way more painful and darker days.

All of us would.

Chapter Sixteen

MEECH

I didn't sleep much that night at all. I let London sleep as I lounged on the chaise drinking my miseries away and watching reruns of Love and Hip Hop, wishing I had these niggas' petty-ass problems.

I couldn't believe that Siren had had the nerve to act a fool like that, considering what she had done. I was sure that she was at home in disbelief that I still hadn't returned, but she needed to realize that our relationship was definitely over, and there was no threatening she could do to get me back.

"What time is it?"

London's voice brought me out of my thoughts. She was standing in the entryway of the bedroom area, leaning against the wall. Exhaustion was giving her such an innocent, appealing look. The black maxi dress that she'd fallen asleep in was wrinkled. Her thigh fell out of the high split, giving me a nice peek of a little bit of booty cheek.

My dick grew hard as cement.

I glanced at my phone and told her, "Five o'clock."

I had gotten comfortable, stripping down to only my boxers, as soon as Siren left. So, I caught London acting as if she wasn't staring. She was obviously caught off guard by finally seeing the chest in flesh that she had laid her head on a few times. I was almost as light-skinned as she was, just a shade or two darker. So even with the lights off, the definition of my chest was evident and was illuminated by the light of the television screen. I prided myself on keeping my body in shape. So, I knew she was admiring the way that my body was cut up like a football player's with the big thighs and calves to match.

"You never went to sleep?" she asked, fighting to keep her eyes on mine and not my body.

Man, it was crazy how much passion I felt just looking into this girl's eyes. As my eyes bore into hers, I wondered if she felt the same.

"I couldn't," I answered. She looked at me sympathetically, so I added, "It's hard to sleep with a hard dick."

She giggled as she rushed toward me, apologizing, "I'm sorry."

As she straddled me, I told her, "No, you're not."

"I passed out. Stop getting me so drunk."

I pushed my lips to the side as if I didn't believe her sincerity. "Mmm humph."

She tried to kiss my cheek. I blocked it and her mouth fell open.

Her lip poked out as she insisted, "I'm sorry, Meech."

I lowered my eyes seductively and ordered, "Show me."

She smiled brightly, happy to oblige. She left my lap, stood next to the chaise, and pulled her dress over her head, revealing a beautiful cream colored mountain of curves, dips, and imperfections that were perfectly placed.

Fuck, I said to myself as I admired the fact that she didn't have on panties or a bra. Now exposed were perky 36 D titties and a bald pussy that I couldn't wait to put my face in.

She stared intensely into my eyes as she used the rubber band around her wrist to pull her locs into a high bun. Then her wide hips slowly switched in front of me. She brought her knees to the chaise and crawled until she was hovering above my crotch.

"Take these off," she demanded as she pulled at my boxers. "I'll help you."

I lifted my ass slightly off of the chaise so that she could pull them down. My dick leaped out, hitting my stomach with a thud, and she stared at it with wide eyes.

When she finally gave me eye contact, I smirked. "You better take all this dick too."

She didn't say anything. She just grabbed the back of my neck and kissed me like I didn't even know I liked to be kissed. Then she left my mouth and started traveling down my body with licks and kisses. She wrapped her hands around my dick, licked the tip teasingly, and then took me all in with one fell swoop. She was aggressively jagging my dick as she sucked it in and out of her throat, gagging and spitting like a fucking porn star.

That shit was incredible.

I felt like a bitch because of the way my eyes squeezed shut tightly and my toes curled. I hadn't had passion and anticipation in a long time, though. This shit was different, and it was just what I needed to get my mind off of the bullshit.

"Come here." I had to stop her. If she had gone any longer, I would've burst in her mouth.

She smiled, happy that she had obviously pleased me beyond my expectations. As she straddled me, I reached down for my shorts, reached into the pocket and got one of the condoms.

I couldn't rip that package open and slide that Magnum on fast enough. My dick was already pulsating and leaking with precum. I knew that this would be a fast nut, but I would get her back with a long, hurt-so-good second round.

She stood on her tip toes, positioned herself above my thick, nine inches, and slid down. The massive moisture inside of her pussy was like a wet blanket that wrapped tightly around my dick as she bounced up and down on it.

My head fell back against the chaise as my hands held her waist. I guided my dick as far into that pussy as it wished to be. Then she bent over, put her face into my neck, and started to molest it with her tongue as she rode me.

This shit was different. We weren't fucking. I dared not say we were making love, but this slow, passionate intimacy was far from some random fucking.

I was so far deep into her cozy pussy that I felt like my dick was lost. I was fighting my way into her body, as deep as I wanted to go, and she was whimpering and moaning out as I hit every spot along the way.

"Fuck!" I grunted.

Just like I figured, I was cumming already. She knew it too. She left my neck, sat straight up, clenched her inner muscles and bounced up and down, hard and fast until all of my frustrations were spilling out into the condom.

"Arrrrgh!" I came so hard that I gripped her waist, making her ride stop as my eyes squeezed shut. "Shit!"

I finally opened my eyes and a smiling, amused London was in full view.

"Don't laugh," I told her. "It's been a long time."

She smirked. "Mmm humph."

"I'm serious," I insisted. "I'ma show yo' ass how I get down soon as you get this dick hard again. Just let me take a leak."

When I attempted to rise up, she used her weight to stop me. "Wait. I have a confession to make."

Oh shit, I thought.

I wondered what the hell she could have to tell me. She could've been getting ready to tell me anything. A post-sex confession couldn't have been good.

She bit her bottom lip anxiously and avoided my eyes as she said, "I like you."

I was relieved and my smile showed it.

"No, I really do," she added. "We haven't known each other that long, but I don't know...I feel...*something*. You're cool, real, caring, and considerate. Niggas out here ain't like that. And I...I hope that you weren't just spending all of that time with me to get this." Then she looked down to where she was still sitting on my dick.

On the outside, I grinned. Shit, I was actually blushing. But on the inside, I felt like shit. She'd said I was real, when I hadn't been a hundred percent real with her at all.

I swallowed the guilt and said, "I got you, shorty. I fucks with you more than you know. It wasn't just about getting some pussy. But it was good as fuck, and I plan on getting it a lot." She giggled as I added, "I see the same qualities in you that you see in me. I'm feeling you too."

As she smiled with contentment, I tapped her ass, motioning for her to get up. She did, and I hopped up, walking into the bathroom a few feet away feeling like a million bucks.

Just as I pulled the condom off of my dick and flushed it, loud banging filled the air. I ripped the door open and saw a frantic London looking at me curiously.

"Who is that?" she asked as she threw on her dress.

"I don't know." I hurried over to my shorts and threw them on, skipping the boxers. "Maybe it's housekeeping or some shit. Let me go check."

As I ran down the steps, it finally dawned on me.

If that bitch, Siren, came back, I'm fucking her up!

Really, I was. I was gon' fuck her up like she was a nigga on the street. Dead ass.

I finally reached the door and when I ripped it open, sure enough, it was Siren's bat-shit, crazy, psycho ass.

Stupid, I thought to myself. I was stupid as fuck to even believe that I had scared her enough to keep her from coming back. Obviously, no matter how crazy I was acting, she was going to out crazy me.

She was real caught off guard by my appearance. She stared at my bare chest in disgust.

"*Really?*" finally came bellowing from her mouth so loud that I was sure she could be heard in the lobby. So, I snatched her ass up. Forgetting about London, I yanked her into the suite with her fighting against me, swinging, scratching, and cursing.

"You ain't shit! I hate you!"

"Shut the fuck up!" My rage was just as fiery as hers as I hemmed her up against the wall by the collar of her shirt. "I told yo' ass I don't fuck with you!" I growled. "Didn't I tell yo' ass not to come back?"

Her brown skin was red with rage. Tears streamed down her face. She had on a wrinkled t-shirt and even more wrinkled jogging pants with flips flops. It looked like she had suddenly decided to come shit on my good time and just threw on whatever. She was a mess. She looked like a broken-hearted woman, but I knew that her heartbreak wasn't because the man she loved was with another woman. I didn't see love in her eyes at all. This shit was a game to her. I was just somebody that took care of her that she didn't want to lose.

SIREN

I was hurt. All these years, I'd yearned for a man to love and take care of me the way that Meech already was. I didn't appreciate him until it was seemingly too late. I was too exhausted because of that realization to even fight him as he screamed into my face, jaws clenched and mouth fuming like a raging pit bull.

But I was just as enraged as he was. I had gone through his phone the day before while he was asleep. I tiptoed into the room, tipped out, and went through the phone within ten minutes before returning it to the nightstand next to his bed without him knowing. I saw all of their text messages, the pictures she'd sent him, and the mushy shit they had said to one another. That's why, when he left out last night, I followed their asses to SLR and then to Aura Suites.

When he'd made me leave last night, I knew that if I wanted any chance to stay in his life, I had to leave. But as I lay in bed, waiting for him to come home and he never did, I refused to let him layup with this bitch and fall for her even more than he already had.

I had to put a stop to this shit ASAP. I figured that I would only be securing my fate as a homeless single mother, but if I couldn't have him, this bitch couldn't either.

"Fuck that! I'm not gon' let you do this!" I shouted.

"*Let me?*"

He shook his head in disbelief. As he did, something on the stairs caught his eye. I looked into the direction that he was staring and saw the same chick from the Loca Lounge. It was the same chick that I'd fucked up, and the same chick that had sent him numerous pics. She was standing on the stairs glaring at Meech in disbelief. It was only then that his anger subsided and he let me go, assumingly not wanting to appear like a monster in her presence.

When I saw the cut that I'd engraved across her cheek, I chuckled devilishly, and that's when I'd stupidly caught her attention. When she saw my face, I became her main focus as she stormed down the carpeted stairs with her purse over her shoulders.

"Bae…" He called for her so lovingly that the compassion in his voice made my heart rip into pieces.

My head whipped around like a possessed demon. "*Bae?*"

He glared a hole through my fucking head, and just as he was about to race toward me, we were ambushed by London.

She swung on me and screamed, "You're the bitch that jumped me!"

I hated that she recognized me. The last thing I wanted Meech to know was that I had jumped his precious new boo. My heart sank as I stepped back, dodging her wild swings while Meech fought to contain her.

"You stupid-ass bitch! Let me go, Meech! *Let me go*!"

He calmly told her, "I'm not letting you go, baby," in a tone that I hadn't heard him use toward me in...shit...*years*.

That's when I knew I really had to get rid of this bitch for good, so I said, "You gawd damn right, I jumped you! You shouldn't be fucking my man!"

"I'm not with her," Meech told her as she continued to wrestle inside of his bear hug.

"We live together!" I shouted. "Have you ever been to his house, boo? Think about it!"

Immediately, she stopped fighting and looked into Meech's eyes, which were full of remorse.

I stood against the wall with my arms folded, glaring at them as they had this sad-ass exchange.

All of a sudden, there was a round of hard knocks on the door. Then a man's voice announced, "Security!"

Meech had no other choice but to let London go. He reluctantly released her and opened the door. London looked like she wanted to take this as an opportunity to fight me, but she was mindful of the presence of security.

Instead, she rushed through the open door, past Meech and security, spewing, "Fuck you, Meech."

Meech moved to go after her, but the security guard stepped in his way, blocking him. Meech didn't fight his way past security as the guard peered through the doorway. When he saw me standing against the wall, he obviously assessed the scene and assumed what had happened. "There was a report of loud noise coming from this suite. Is everything okay?" he asked me.

When I smiled and said, "Now it is," Meech rolled his eyes at me as he bit his lip in anger.

"Okay," the security guard responded. "Please gather your things and leave the premises. I'll give you all a minute to get ready."

Meech didn't say a word as he turned and went up the stairs. But I wasn't through with him, so I followed him as the security guard stood in the doorway, keeping his eye on us.

"I know you're not in your feelings over a bitch you just met." I was on his heels, but my voice was at a minimum to avoid alerting security.

"Get the fuck away from me," was all that he said, but I knew that he was indeed in his feelings. As he picked up his wallet, keys, threw on his shirt, and picked up his boxers, there was the saddest look on his face. He was more sad that she was gone than he was mad at me. Her leaving had sucked all fight from him. That meant she was one powerful bitch.

I followed him again as he headed down the stairs. He walked straight past security, out into the parking lot and up to the driver's side of his Lexus.

"You're mad at me about a mistake I made over six years ago, but you are lying and being disloyal *right now*."

His jaw clenched as he popped the lock. "Get the fuck away from me, wit' yo crazy ass."

"Where you goin'?" I asked as I folded my arms across my chest. "To chase that bitch?"

As he climbed into the car without a word, I swore to him, "I'm not going anywhere, Meech. I'm not gon' let you leave me!" As he slammed the door, I raised my voice, "It's not worth it!" As he put the car in reverse and started to back up, I smacked my hands against the window. "You hear me? I'm not letting you leave me because of this, Meech!"

He pulled off, and I knew that I couldn't chase his truck in flip flops. I finally stopped and just watched him pull out of the lot, praying that I hadn't lost him forever.

Just as his truck was no longer in view, my shoulders hunched in defeat. Before I could mope towards my car, I was being attacked from the back!

I felt a hard blow to the back of my head as I heard a female scream, "Bitch, you thought it was over?"

The blow and weight of her body had sent me to the pavement. I was so caught off guard that I was barely fighting back. She was on top of me, punching my face, clawing at it, grabbing my hair and banging my head against the pavement!

"Bitch, you cut me!"

"Get the fuck off of me!"

"I'ma fuck you up, you fat ass bitch!"

We were screaming and clawing at one another! I was swinging back in defense, but honestly, from jump she had the upper hand. I was never able to effectively defend myself against her powerful blows, which I was sure were leaving me bloody, black and blue.

"You lucky I ain't got no knife! Otherwise, I'd show you how to cut a bitch!"

"Fuck you!" I spat. She was clawing at my fucking eyes! "Arrrgh!"

I was attempting to use my legs to push her off of me. At first, I had no luck. But then, suddenly I felt her weight lifting off of my body, but my weave was entangled in her fingers.

"Let me go, bitch!" I shouted. I took my own hair in my hands and attempted to pull against her in order to get free.

When I heard a male voice order, "Let her go," my heart skipped a beat. I hoped Meech had come back, but when they finally came into view, I saw that it was the same security guard who'd come to the room. He was dragging her away as she fought to get free from his grasp.

She kicked and screamed as she spewed, "Fuck you, bitch! You can have his ass! Keep him!"

But as I scrambled to my feet and towards my car, I knew that that was a gawd damn lie. Something told me that, no matter how hard I had tried to break them apart, neither she nor Meech were truly done with each other.

DOLLA

I had to tell Meagan about Jada and my other kids while I had the courage. After I burst in her mouth and managed to leave without an argument, I went home and laid next to Jada feeling like shit. Cheating was one thing. Jada was always disappointed when she found about that I had cheated, but she always eventually got over it. However, kids outside of our relationship would kill her emotionally and send her to a point of no return. I knew that she would take my kids and never come back, so I didn't have the courage to tell her yet. I had to keep it real with Meagan in order to buy myself some more time.

So the next day, on a warm, Tuesday morning, after dropping the kids off at school, I made my way to her condo, ready to piss off yet another woman.

"So what do you have to talk to me about?" Meagan sat next to me holding Brandon.

Her curly hair was back in a ponytail and she was wearing her glasses. Between tending to the twins, she had been attempting to do homework for the online courses she'd been taking this semester since she wasn't able to attend classes on campus due to the birth of the twins.

I was cradling Bianca to my chest. I was thankful that the twins were with us, ensuring that Meagan couldn't get violent with me.

She looked at me like I was crazy as my mouth opened and closed without any words coming out.

"What?" she urged.

I sighed heavily, "Fuck it. I'm just going to say it." I paused, fighting the urge to chicken out. "I don't want to be in a relationship with you because...I am in a relationship with someone else." Meagan chuckled in a way that I couldn't identify as I added, "We've been in a relationship for nine years—"

Her laughter got louder, interrupting me. "I knew it!"

My eyebrows rose, wondering what kind of psychotic response this was, as tears paired with her laughter.

"It was so obvious," she said as she wiped away a runaway tear. "After I got pregnant, you started treating me so bad that I knew it had to be another woman."

She chuckled sarcastically. "You act like a married nigga, and after nine years, you might as well be one."

Meagan was obviously hurt, but she at least wasn't raging mad, so I was a little relieved. Though a few slow, silent tears fell from her eyes, she was surprisingly way calmer than I assumed she would be.

"If you thought I was in a relationship already, what was up with all of the pressure that you were putting on me to be with you?" I asked her.

"I assumed that you were in a relationship, but I hoped I was wrong. I mean, we had only been fucking for three months before I got pregnant. We weren't in love, so I'm not super hurt that you don't want to be with me. But it would be nice, especially for the babies. But if we can't, then..." She simply shrugged.

I knew her ass didn't really like me like that.

"Nine years is a long time. Y'all got any kids?" she asked.

"Yeah," I sighed. "Two. Brittany and...*Brandon*."

"*What?*" She squealed so loud that both babies jumped. Then she actually chuckled. "Why would you let me name him Brandon when you already had a kid by that name?"

I laughed only because she was as well now. "I tried to talk you out of it. You wouldn't listen."

She shook her head. "That's a damn shame. But thanks for finally telling me."

I was still in awe at how easily this had gone. Right then I knew that I had been right. She only wanted to be with me because I didn't want to be with her. Even though she had said that it would've been nice, a woman who *really* wanted to be with me would be sitting here fighting for me, like Jada always had.

"I had to tell you," I replied. "Trying to split my time between business, home, and here is causing a lot of drama in my household. Plus, it's becoming obvious to her that I'm up to something, so I need you to understand that I can't be over here real late at night, and I can't answer every phone call, until I tell her."

"When are you going to tell her?"

Just the thought made me cringe. I ran my hands over my head in frustration. "I will...*one day.*" We both laughed again.

"Seriously," I insisted. "One day, I will. I owe you and the twins that much."

CHAPTER SEVENTEEN

DOLLA

After leaving Meagan's crib, I felt like a weight had been lifted off of me. Everything wasn't squared away, but at least it was a start to stopping some of the drama. This motivated me to throw the shit directly at the fan. It was time to holla at King so that the rest of my life could be drama and stress free as well.

I had already called King and set up a time to meet in the office of the convenience store.

Then I called Meech. I wanted him to be there when I talked to King so that he could know just what type of bitch he had living under his roof. I was sure that it was Siren who put the solo idea in his head, and I figured he would rethink the way he'd been acting if he knew the truth about her.

"What up, tho?" When Meech answered, he sounded like he was in the same fucked up mood he'd been in lately.

At this time of morning, I expected to be waking him up, but this nigga sounded wide awake and angry. I could hear in his background that he was already in the streets as well.

"Damn, bruh. What's wrong with you?"

He groaned before answering, "Man, this bitch, Siren, is psycho as fuck."

You don't fucking say. "What did she do now?"

"She showed up at the telly acting a fucking fool."

"The telly? Who were you there with?"

"Some chick I met at Loca like two weeks ago. I was kinda feeling shorty too, but now she won't even answer the phone. I don't even know how she got to the crib because she rode with me, but she walked out and security wouldn't let me follow her. I drove around everywhere looking for her."

"*Security*? Damn, it was that bad?"

He huffed, saying, "Yeah, it was rough. I may have to go ahead and let her move out with Elijah. I don't want to, though. I like seeing my son every day. I don't trust that I can kick her out and she won't try to retaliate in some kinda way, either. She knows too much."

Speaking of which. "True. Well, I was calling to see if you were available to meet up."

"Yeah. Something up?"

"A lot is up. I need to talk to you and King together. Can you be at the store in twenty?"

"Yeah." Before hanging up, he added, "Aye, you heard from Brooklyn today?"

"Nah. Why? What's up?"

"Nothing major. Just been hitting his phone all morning with no answer."

"Shit. It's only ten o'clock. Maybe the nigga's still sleep."

"Could be. A'ight. I'll see you in a minute."

When he hung up, I wondered what the fuck we were going to do with Siren because Meech was right. She knew too damn much. There were too many thirsty niggas in these streets. All it would take was for her vindictive ass to meet one of them and tell them everything.

****

Twenty minutes later, King and Meech were staring at me impatiently as I stood against the wall in the office with my hands in my pockets, forcing myself to say the words that were about to shake up an organization that had run so perfectly for years. Kennedy was King's everything, and although Meech was pissed with Siren right now, she was still his girl. So I wasn't sure if King's response would sit right with Meech, causing even more tension between us.

"Sooo," I started hesitantly. "I need to tell y'all some shit that's gon' piss y'all off, but I need you to hear me out so that we can fix this shit."

Both Meech and King sat up a bit more in their seats saying in unison, "Okay."

With a deep breath, I just chose to spit it out. "Meech, after you kicked Siren out and told Jada to go look for her, Jada saw her talking real cozy with this detective chick." They both stared at me with eyes full of questions, but I just kept talking over their silent confusion. "When Siren saw Jada, she and the detective immediately went in different directions, so Jada knew something was up. Siren got in the car and Jada started drilling her, but the shit Siren was saying wasn't sounding right to Jada. Seeing her with the detective made her think that she was the one that gave them that tip about the van, so she got pissed. She pulled into an alley, and they got into it. Siren jumped out. Jada felt like Siren was guilty and couldn't be trusted, so she jumped out after Siren and shot her."

Meech's mouth flew open, and King's eyes bucked.

"Yeah, Jada shot Siren," I admitted. "She wasn't robbed."

"The fuck?" King asked, with a bit of humor behind it.

Surprisingly, Meech was just shaking his head like the shit was unbelievable. I thought he'd have more of an emotional reaction to his girl possibly talking to the cops and her best friend trying to kill her. His nonchalant reaction made him more suspect in my eyes.

But that was a talk for later. Then, I laid the rest on them. "But when we got to the hospital, Siren swore to Jada that she wasn't talking to the cops. She said that the detective has been stalking her, trying to threaten her with some jail time if she didn't give her something on King, and that's the only reason why she was talking to her that day."

King's head cocked to the side. "How long this shit been going on?"

"She said for years. The detective pulled her over the day Kayla was born, expecting for Meech to be in the car. There were drugs and guns in the car because Siren was

A Thug's Love 2

supposed to have made a drop that day, but Kennedy went into labor. The detective let her go because she agreed to set *you* up."

King's face fell in his hands with a sigh. Meech stared blankly at the wall, asking, "So that bitch has been talking to the cops since she been with me?" It was like he was asking himself that question and shook his head sadly at the answer that he already knew.

"You sure you ain't know about this?" King asked him.

I silently agreed with his concern. Meech had been acting shady as fuck lately, and King and I both looked at him just like he had been acting: suspect.

Meech looked from me to King in disbelief as we sat in silence. It seemed as if he couldn't believe that we would even think it was a possibility. "Are you niggas serious?"

"Dead ass," King answered calmly.

Again, Meech looked from me to King in disbelief, saying, "Tricking on y'all is tricking on *me*!"

"Not if you cut a deal," King told him. "And you been walking around this ma'fucka lately like you got a lot of things on your mind. Is turning state one of 'em?"

Meech couldn't believe it. The heavy blow of King's audacity caused Meech to fall back in his seat and just stare at King.

"I'ma let you slide with that, nigga," Meech told King. "But watch your mouth. I helped you build this motherfucka, so I ain't gon' help tear it down. I for damn sure ain't gon' take food out of my son's mouth just to keep from facing time. I ain't built like that."

King just stared at him. I knew that, deep down, King knew that Meech was telling the truth. I did too. I saw it in his eyes. This dude was our brother, our partner. He just wasn't made that way.

Meech tore his eyes away from King and continued to stare blankly at the wall.

I sighed deeply, preparing myself to fuck their heads up even more. "Siren swears that she hasn't told the cops shit...*recently.*" That got both Meech and King's attention. "But at first, the detective was on her hard. She was scared that if she didn't say something, she or you, Meech, would wind up in jail. So she gave the detective a heads up on a drop we were making three years ago. It was the drop that King was supposed to make—"

Immediately, they knew what I was saying to them. Their groans and sighs were so loud that they overpowered my words. King slumped down in his seat with his hands over his head. Meech just shook his head with his eyes full of disbelief.

King was literally growling in anger as he asked, "So *Siren* is the reason why Kennedy got locked up?"

Reluctantly, I nodded slowly. As King looked to the ceiling and bit his lip, I told him, "Me and Jada didn't want to say anything until after the wedding so y'all could enjoy it, but now—"

"We gotta do something," Meech said without hesitation.

That shocked the shit outta me. I had expected him to be a little less understanding about this, considering that Siren was his woman and the mother of his child.

"Yeah, we do," King added. "She gots to go. We gotta kill her."

Although Meech was understanding, he wasn't down with that shit, though. "Kill her? Hold on, man."

King spun his head around and glared at Meech. "Nigga, is you crazy? She talkin' to the cops—"

"She said she hasn't said shit else. *If* she had, we'd all be in prison right now. The police would've raided every spot by now!"

"So!" King barked. "The bitch put Kennedy in prison! She gots to go! We've killed ma'fuckas for doing less! She's dead! And you gon' be the one to kill her since you in the house with her!"

King was obviously testing Meech to see where his loyalty lied, since Meech had been so questionable recently. It was a fucked up way of testing him, though.

Meech jumped to his feet and stood over King, his jaw clenched with anger. "You expect me to kill my girl, Elijah's mother, nigga? Really? You really don't give a fuck about nobody but you and Kennedy, huh?!"

King jumped to his feet as well. He and Meech were eye-to-eye, standing so close to one another that they were breathing each other's oxygen. Suddenly, this small-ass office felt even tinier, and I was just a fly on the wall. I felt King's rage, but shit, I felt Meech's too.

MEECH

"You expect me to kill my girl, Elijah's mother, nigga? Really? You really don't give a fuck about nobody but you and Kennedy, huh?!" I couldn't believe this nigga.

True, this shit was fucked up. I hated Siren even worse now than I had before. Now I knew that the bitch had been dirty the entire time I was with her ass. But kill her, I couldn't do. She was Elijah's mother, and little did this nigga know, she was *his* baby's mother.

This nigga had no compassion, though. All he could think about was Kennedy spending three years away from of us, and it being the fault of a bitch that ate at the table with us and got money with us the whole time she was gone.

"What? You a ghost, nigga?" he asked me.

"Ghost?" I questioned with a glare.

"You ain't got no heart?"

I chuckled sarcastically, waving my hand, dismissing this clown. "Man, fuck you."

Our anger was bringing us closer and closer into one another's space. Our eyes were glaring fiery rage into one another's as our noses flared and our jaws tightened.

"You want me to kill my bitch over your bitch?" I asked him mockingly. "I know you don't give two fucks about Siren, but *Elijah* does, and he's my fucking son. He means just as much to me as Kennedy ever did to you, nigga."

I felt myself getting way too emotional, so I bowed my head, ran my hand over my face, and walked toward the door. "Figure out another way to take care of this, and holla at me when you do."

As I walked out of the office, I knew that Siren's time on this earth was short. She had committed the ultimate sin against King's precious queen. And no matter her ties to us, he would never let anyone get away with that with any punishment other than death. There was no other way. The risk was otherwise too great. However, if I allowed King to kill Siren, knowing that Elijah was his son, he wouldn't forgive me either.

Plus, the way the nigga was looking at me let me know that he thought I was on some shady shit. My attitude lately had been real suspect, so I couldn't blame him. But regardless of his disloyalty to me, I never wanted the nigga to think that I would fuck up my money or what we had built. This drug game was way more complex, and I never wanted to look suspect to anyone in it, no matter their disloyalty to me.

It was time to tell him.

MARIA

The music in Carnivale was loud. Summer was starting to take over the spring air, so the restaurant in Chicago's west loop was lively. It had such a festive vibe with Latin music playing as patrons drank and ate Latin cuisine.

It was the perfect atmosphere for a celebration.

"Congratulations, Maria." Detective Jefferies lifted his shot glass with a smile.

I grinned saying, "Congratulations to you too."

Then we toasted and gulped down our shots of tequila.

This was definitely a celebration. Detective Jefferies had gone undercover last night to make the buy with Brooklyn. It resulted in Brooklyn's arrest. He was now facing so many years that he wouldn't get out in time to see his two-year-old daughter get married or have children. Besides the one hundred bricks of cocaine that we'd arrested him with, the stupid motherfucker had had the nerve to have guns in the trunk too. We had run ballistics on all of them, and one came back with a body on it. The state's attorney was now trying to convince him to help us with the case against King in exchange for an extremely lighter sentence.

Yet, I knew it wouldn't take much convincing at all.

After so many years, I was *finally* about to snatch King off of his throne.

CHAPTER EIGHTEEN

MEECH

After leaving the store, I went to Loca Lounge for two reasons. I needed a hard drink before confronting King, and I wanted to grill Tangi about London. She hadn't been answering my calls since she stormed out of the door of the suite. I had even gone by her mother's house. No one answered, and since London didn't have a car, there was no way for me to tell whether anyone was really home or not. I was hoping that she would be sitting in her usual seat at the bar. When I walked in and didn't see that phat 'ol ass hanging off the back of that bar stool, my heart actually sank. I realized then how much I really liked that girl.

I knew that I should've pushed that fucking, scrawny security guard the fuck outta my way and chased her down, but I had allowed Siren's dramatics to wear me out.

Unfortunately, there was another bartender behind the bar. Tangi's shift didn't start this early, so I knocked back a few shots, paid my tab, and called King on my way out. As I waited for him to answer, I hoped that his ass had calmed down. Whether he had or not, I didn't give a fuck. We were about to have this out.

When he answered with a simple and dry, "Yo," I knew that he was still pissed and ready to put a bullet in Siren's head, and had the audacity to still be looking at me suspiciously.

This motherfucker thought I was disloyal when he had been disloyal from the fucking gate.

"I need to talk to you *alone*. Without Dolla...just you and me."

"I'm at the crib. Come through."

"On my way."

****

King barely made eye contact as I followed him into his crib. As he closed the door, I asked, "Where's Kennedy?"

He looked at me with a look that asked why I gave a fuck, but he dryly told me, "Grocery shopping."

"Let's sit on the patio," I told him. "I need to smoke."

Liquor wasn't enough. I needed some loud to ease the stress of this conversation.

We walked through the kitchen and sliding door onto the platform deck, and sat on the cushioned bench. It was beginning to be a beautiful day, weather-wise. It was almost June, so at one in the afternoon, it was already seventy-five degrees and sunny. It was a shame that I felt like a massive, dangerous storm was brewing between me and King as we sat silently on the bench while I sparked my blunt.

King's face was cold, calculating, and menacing as he stared out onto his well-manicured lawn. I knew that he was thinking about the three years that he had spent without the love of his life while she was in that hellhole away from Kayla. I also knew that he was fuming with anticipation to make Siren pay.

"I know what you're thinking, and I don't blame you," I told him calmly. "If it were my girl, I would feel the same way. Shit, had it been Siren, I would feel the same way." I didn't even look at King as I took a long pull of the weed. I didn't even know if he was looking at me or paying attention. I just knew that he was still sitting there. "You're right for wanting to kill her, and you were right, I have been acting shady as fuck. But you were wrong at the same time for considering any of it. You can't kill Siren for a good reason, and I've been acting shady for the same reason. I found out that *you're* Elijah's father."

I felt his body jerk and his eyes burning a hole through the side of my head, but I couldn't even look at the nigga. I couldn't look at the nigga who I thought was my ride or fucking die. I had never expected this nigga to betray me. But he was the same nigga who had just accused me with disgust of being the exact nigga that he was.

"I know you didn't know, but you *did* know that you had fucked her when I came to you and Dolla to tell y'all I wanted to get with her. You didn't tell me shit, though."

Through my peripheral vision, I saw his body slump as he leaned back against the bricks of the house.

"Man," he sighed. "I...I...Real talk, I just didn't give a fuck about her like that. She's like family. She's cool. She was loyal, I thought, but I never wanted her in that way. She didn't want anyone to know that we had slept together because I was in a relationship at the time, so I didn't say shit, even when you mentioned it. That was in loyalty to her, I guess, and I didn't want Kennedy to know. It had nothing to do with you. That was fucked up, though, I know. I can't say shit but I'm sorry, my nigga. I never fucked her again after you wifed her, and I swear to God that that's the only time I ever lied to you."

I just nodded and kept smoking, staring at the flowers in the potted plant on the patio. I still couldn't look at the nigga. Although he sounded sincere, he was just as sincere when watching me love this girl, knowing that they both were keeping a secret from me.

"She's sure he's mine?"

"I'm sure. Y'all got the same birthmark." I heard him sigh heavily as I continued. "Plus, Eric said he never even fucked Siren. She told me that she used Eric as a scapegoat because you had just proposed to Tiana and she knew you would tell her to get rid of it. She wanted her baby, so she lied."

Again, he sighed. I saw his hands go up to his face. I had never seen the nigga so silent. Usually, he always had a plan or knew what to say. The nigga always knew how to fix shit. But this was something he couldn't finagle. He couldn't kill a nigga to fix this. There wasn't shit he could do but deal.

"I know that you got a lot to think about and consider, especially considering how and when to break this shit to Kennedy. But I know you. Now that you know, you're going to be a good father to him."

"Of course," King didn't hesitate to say.

That's when I finally looked him in the eyes. I wanted him to see how sincere I was. I saw the anguish in his eyes, but I wanted him to see the desperation in mine as I said, "Just let me remain in his life, man. I know I've only been with him for a few years, but that's..." I stopped. I felt my throat tightening and my eyes stinging. My voice cracked as I forced out, "That's my son too."

We were two bitches out there, with tears in our eyes and shit. But we were men who, aside from all of the bullshit, wanted to be a good father to a kid because he deserved it.

"You don't have to ask me that," he told me. "Whatever you want."

Fighting back tears so hard that our jaws were tight, he reached his hand out to shake mine, and I shook his out of respect for the man who was my son's father.

I still didn't know how our personal relationship would be. But we had built an empire like no other, and had a son that we also needed to raise into a man. Both of which I needed to join forces with King to protect.

So, for now, I would just play my part.

KENNEDY

A number that I didn't recognize had called my phone twice already that day. I hadn't had the phone for even three whole weeks, so I figured it was a telemarketer. I ignored the call for a third time while pulling into the driveway of my home.

Just as I was about to call King and ask him to come help me carry the groceries inside, I got yet another call. This time, it was from Logan Correctional Facility, so I answered, immediately pressing zero and expecting to hear either Ms. Jerry or Dre's voice, but it was neither.

"Hello?"

"Kennedy..."

Seconds later, I hyperventilated after hearing what the caller had to say. I could hardly breathe or get out of the car. After ending the call, I walked into the house in a daze, not even caring about the fucking groceries anymore. I walked into the house in a fog. The caller's words were still ringing in my brain. I walked into the den looking for King, desperately needing his arms around me, but he wasn't there. I went upstairs and he wasn't in bed. I walked back down the stairs, figuring that he must be in the living room, but he wasn't there either. Desperately, I rushed through the kitchen, resting my phone on the island. From where I stood, I could see King's Balmain sneakers as he sat on the bench. I started to rush out of the patio doors, until I heard him talking to someone, so I hesitated.

"I've been acting shady for the same reason. I found out that *you're* Elijah's father. I know you didn't know, but you *did* know that you had fucked her when I came to you and Dolla to tell y'all I wanted to get with her. You didn't tell me shit, though."

I was sure that it was Meech's voice that I'd heard, but I just knew that I hadn't heard him correctly.

I *couldn't* have.

I figured that I had heard wrong, or that hopefully Meech was talking to someone else that I didn't know was out there.

Maybe he's on the phone. Maybe someone else is outside, I thought as my heart began to pound out of my chest and I fought for breath.

There was silence for a few seconds. I stood still as a statue outside of the patio door, regretting what else I would hear.

Then I silently gasped as I heard King sadly say, "Man." Then he sighed, and I grasped at my chest. My heart had already been broken that day and something told me that it was about to be ripped out of my chest for good. "I...I...Real talk, I just didn't give a fuck about her like that. She's like family." My hand flew over my mouth to silence my wail. I used my free hand to grasp onto the kitchen island to prevent myself from losing my balance as I felt myself about to faint at any moment. "...I swear to God that that's the only time I ever lied to you."

But was it the only time he ever lied to *me*?

My knees buckled and met the cold Mother of Pearl tile. My hands clawed at it as the pain became so unbearable that I just wanted to die. I could still hear their voices, but they sounded like muffles underneath the sound of my heart breaking.

In minutes, my life had been changed from sunshine to a tornado of hurt that was going to suck me up and kick me with its wrath. I hadn't been out of prison for three weeks, but yet, I now wanted to go back. I'd hated being there, but I would switch this pain for that anxiety because at least then, there had been some light. At least then I knew that on May 13th, I would feel better and I would be free. But kneeling on my kitchen floor, I didn't foresee me ever healing from this or ever being free from the heartache.

I have to go.

I had to get out of there. I *had* to go, so I forced myself to my feet and ran upstairs, allowing my tears to fall along the way.

KING

This shit was beyond crazy. It was life-changing. I had a son with Siren. Things were different now. I now was thinking twice about killing her. I knew that my days were numbered because Kennedy was for sure going to kill me whenever she found out.

This shit was bad...*real* bad.

So for about an hour, Meech and I sat out on the patio talking about Elijah, Siren, what to do, and how to do it. Afterwards, we were still lost with no solutions. The only thing that we were positive about was that he wanted to introduce Elijah to his real father. Elijah knew that Meech wasn't his biological father, so he had questioned it every now and then, especially on Father's Day. Meech was eager to let him know that his biological father was eager to meet him. He just didn't know that he already knew him. Uncle King was actually Daddy, and even as I walked Meech to the door, I still couldn't believe it. As I shook up with Meech, I apologized again for even thinking that he would betray us, with the disbelief of all of this in the front of my mind. Each time I had played around with Elijah throughout these years, each time that I told him he couldn't play Madden with us, each time that I told him that he was too young to hang out with us, I 'd been talking to my son.

My son.

Meech and I had agreed to talk the next day, giving me sometime to marinate on all of this shit. I closed the door with a heavy heart. This emotional roller coaster was exhausting. I'd gone from happy, to enraged, to somber all in a matter of hours. I just wanted to go upstairs, lay across the bed, and wait for Kennedy to come home.

Even the thought of Kennedy left me sick as fuck. The girl had gone to prison for me. Because of how loyal and loving I was to her, she did that shit for me. And now, I had to let her know that it was all in vain. This one action of deceit would drown out the years I had spent committed to her while she was gone, waiting for her...waiting to show her the same love and loyalty that she had shown me.

I entered my bedroom and headed straight for the bed. As I sat on it, kicking my shoes off, handwriting on the mirror caught my attention. Written in red lipstick were the words: *Congratulations! You finally have the son you've always wanted! Fuck you!*

I jumped to my feet and ran downstairs, looking for Kennedy in every room...shit, even in every closet, but I knew better. She wasn't there. As I stood in the kitchen paralyzed with fear, I called her phone and instantly heard my ringtone. I looked around like a madman and finally saw her phone ringing on the island.

"Shit!" I ended the called and immediately called Meech.

"Hello?"

"Aye, was Kennedy outside when you left?"

"No. What's wrong?"

I knew he could hear the desperation in my voice. "She...um...she knows, man. I think she...uh...she must've..." I couldn't even fucking breathe as I paced in the kitchen. "I think she must have heard us or some shit. Her phone is right here in the kitchen."

My eyes closed tight with unbearable grief. I knew her heart was broken, and I just wanted to fix it.

"I need to find her," I insisted.

"Let me see if she called Siren."

"A'ight. Hit me back."

I hung up and called Jada, who hadn't heard from Kennedy since the day before. Then I called her mother. I acted normal, attempting not to alarm her, but she hadn't heard from her either. After hanging up with her mother, a text message came through from Meech saying that Siren hadn't heard from Kennedy at all. I called the daycare center and they said that she had just picked up Kayla, so I calmed down. I assumed that, though she was more than likely pissed and hurt, she was on her way home.

Chapter Nineteen

KING

I sat waiting at the crib for hours. I was just sitting in the living room with the lights off, not knowing what to do. I couldn't eat, sleep or drink. I just sat there praying that Kennedy would show up while I stalked everyone, even her father, hoping that she and Kayla were with one of them. But each time, everyone swore that they hadn't heard from her. And as the sun went down and the living room grew dark, I knew that if she was coming home, she would have by now.

Enraged at my own stupidity, I left, ready to kick down doors to find her and my daughter. I knew she wouldn't be at Meech's house, so I went to Dolla and Jada's first.

"I'm serious! She's not here!" Jada screeched as I gently pushed by her.

I searched every room and closet on the first floor as she called after me.

"King! What's wrong? Calm down!" she shouted at me as she followed me up the stairs.

Again, I searched every room and closet. I even searched the kids' rooms. They looked at me like I was crazy as I searched every inch of their rooms, even under the beds.

"King!" Jada shouted another warning at me as I stormed down the stairs. Again, she was on my heels. "What the fuck is going on? Should I be worried?"

"She's upset," I finally answered. "She overheard something fucked up and I guess she left. She must have forgotten her phone. I can't..." I took a deep breath, still unable to catch it. My fucking head was spinning. "I can't find her, Jada."

"What did she overhear?" Her arms were folded as she glared at me, and I froze. I couldn't even allow the words to leave my throat.

"I gotta go," I said as I went for her front door and flung it open. "Call me if you hear from her, please."

And then I ran to my car without even waiting for her reply.

DOLLA

"He did what?" I asked Jada as I got up to the leave the office of the convenience store.

"He came in here, busting open doors, closets and all kinds of shit!" Jada squealed. "The nigga is spazzing! He can't find Kennedy anywhere."

"You haven't heard from her for real?" I asked.

"No. And she doesn't have her phone. She knows my number by heart, though, so I hope she'll call me."

"A'ight, bae," I told her as I put about a hundred thousand dollars in twenties, fives, and ones inside of the wall safe. "I'll call that nigga to see what's going on. I'll be home in a minute. I'm leaving now."

"Okay."

I hung up, leaving the office and pushing the necessary numbers to call King, when the phone started to ring.

It was Meagan.

"What's up?" I answered, hoping that she hadn't sat on my truth all day and was now stirring in anger.

Yet, instead of anger, I heard tears. "H-Hello? Brandon?"

It wasn't Meagan's voice that I heard. It was her mother's. I stopped dead in my tracks in the middle of the convenience store. The cashier looked at me oddly as I stared blankly, wondering why Meagan's mother would be calling me in tears.

"It's me, Miss Rachel," I told her. "What's wrong?"

"There's..." Her tears made her unable to speak. "T-there's been an...an accident. I need you to come t-to the hospital." Then she broke down in uncontrollable sobs.

I raced out of the store and toward my car.

"Miss Rachel." I was trying to get her attention while I jumped into the car and started it. "Miss Rachel, what happened? What's wrong? Are the babies okay?"

"Yes, they're okay. But...it's Meagan. It's bad. Just come right away. We're at the University of Chicago. Hurry!"

****

Meagan had been in a horrific car accident an hour before her mother called me. She was texting and driving on the expressway and rear ended a semi at seventy miles per hour. Her body was mangled, and she had undergone emergency surgery. There was nothing that the doctors could tell us. As we sat in the waiting room, awaiting some news from the surgeons, we didn't even know if she would survive or not.

At nearly midnight, Meagan was still in surgery. The twins became fussy. Luckily, they had been with their grandmother at the time of the accident.

"Why don't you take them home?"

Not even realizing it, I looked at her like she had lost her damn mind. And that's when I realized that this woman probably didn't even know my situation.

"I can stay here and help you watch them," I insisted.

"They need to go home. They're hungry. I've run out of diapers and milk, and honestly, hearing them cry is just making this worse. I can't tend to them and worry about Meagan..." Then her eyes watered up. "This is just too much... They don't need to be in this hospital with these germs anyway."

I sat there stuck and she looked at me, wondering what the fuck my hesitation was about. Then she started to put their things into the diaper bag. I was still sitting there stuck as she put Brandon, who she was holding, into his car seat.

I didn't want to argue with this woman. She was going through enough. Doctors were trying to save her daughter's life. She was even crying as she took Bianca from me and strapped her into her car seat too.

"Do you need help taking them to the car?" she asked as she wiped tears away. But there was no use. She would wipe some tears away and more would just take their place.

I slowly shook my head and just left like the woman had asked me to.

"I'll call you when I have some news," I heard her say.

"Okay," weakly left my mouth as I carried the twins out.

I walked down the hall, wondering what the fuck to do! I thought maybe I could just take them to Meagan's house because going home was *not* an option. But shit, staying out all night wasn't an option either. Jada had already been texting the hell out of me, wondering where the hell I was, as I'd sat in the hospital for hours.

As I walked through the parking lot, I wracked my brain, trying to come up with a plan. I even thought about taking the twins to one of the girls instead, but last I'd heard, Kennedy was still missing, and then I quickly remembered that Siren was a psychopath that I wasn't desperate enough to allow to help me. As I strapped them into the backseat, I even considered taking them to King or Meech, but they weren't answering their phones.

As I got into the driver's seat, Brandon started to cry, and in response, Bianca did too.

"Fuck!" I shouted at the top of my lungs as I punched the steering wheel. I was angry as I realized that I had no other options.

There wasn't anything that I could do. I had to take them home.

As I reluctantly pulled out of the parking lot, I turned on the radio to drown out my thoughts.

> ♪ *I'm rushing home*
> *She said she's packing her things*
> *And she's leaving the keys to*
> *the front door*
> *Should I have known,*
> *That it would happen once again*
> *Was it something I could've*
> *done to make her stay* ♪

One Chance's lyrics drowned out the twin's cries but only magnified how fucked up this shit was going to be. Jada had been the true, text-book example of a ride or die chick. I had fucked up so much in the past that I could only pray that Jada would find some forgiveness in her heart.

For twenty minutes, I prayed for a miracle. For God to make a way for me to get out of walking into my house with these kids, and when my cell phone rang, displaying Miss Rachel's number, I thought He'd answered my prayers.

"Hel-"

"Oh God!"

But that was far from the case. My prayers had most definitely gone unanswered.

My heart beat with reluctance as I heard the sheer terror and hurt in Miss Rachel's cries. "She's gone! She's gone, Brandon! She didn't make it! Oh my God..."

I cringed as this all became too real. Miss Rachel was crying so desperately that I wanted to turn the car around and console her.

Tears pooled in my eyes as I told her, "I'm coming back." I wasn't trying to avoid taking the kids home. I really wanted to be there for Miss Rachel and I felt like I should be there. Meagan was never my woman, and I didn't love her. But I liked her a lot. She was a good person, and I would truly miss her laugh. She had such a bright future ahead of her. She didn't deserve to die so soon.

Then I thought of my kids, who would never know her, and my heart broke.

"No," Miss Rachel insisted through tears. "I don't want them here. Meagan's father's flight landed a little while ago. He should be here soon, so I won't be alone." Her cries took over her words. She was breaking down yet again. "Jesus! I can't believe she's gone! My babyyyy!" I stayed quiet, listening to her as a tear fell down my cheek. She was able to control her tears enough to say, "Just take care of my grandbabies, Brandon. I have to go."

Just as she hung up, I realized that I was approaching the block that I lived on. I sighed heavily, attempting to gather my composure as I realized the silence. The babies were asleep. As I turned into my driveway, there were no words for how heavy and empty I felt. Meagan was dead, and now I was about to emotionally kill Jada the moment that I walked through the door with these babies. This shit was causing me pain that a nigga like me had never felt before. I had never been so emotionally torn, and I didn't know what to do or how to fix it. But what I did know was that I couldn't sit in that car forever.

I killed the engine as I took a deep breath. "C'mon y'all," I said quietly to the sleeping twins. "Let's go break my baby's heart."

KING

After leaving Jada's crib, I went to Kennedy's parents' homes, doing the same thing—telling them respectfully that I was searching every inch of their house whether they liked it or not, but I never found Kennedy. I knew that she was somewhere hiding from me, but I had checked all of her resources, so where could she be? Shit, as I sat in the car outside of her father's home, I even started calling every major hotel asking if a Kennedy Carter had checked in, but after the tenth hotel, I got nowhere and I was starting feel like a mad man.

So I sat in my car at a gas station near her father's home, not knowing where to go next. I hoped that maybe she had gone back home by now. So I started the car, prepared to just go home, when I felt a constant vibration in my pocket.

My phone was in my hand, so I wondered for a second, then realized that I had shoved Kennedy's phone into my pocket. I frantically reached into my pocket to get it, hoping that she was calling her phone, looking for it. I had her password because I'd set the phone up for her when I bought it. I hoped that she hadn't changed it yet.

She hadn't, so I was able to see the missed calls that had come since I had it. Her mother, father, and Jada had blown her phone up, and the last call was Jada again. However, there was a number that hadn't been stored in the phone that had called quite a few times earlier that day, and then stopped around the time she would have come home and overheard me and Meech. Then I noticed words flashing at the top of the screen, notifying text messages. I scrolled to the inbox and saw that the same unsaved number had texted her around the same time.

773-413-0999: *What's up? It's Dre, baby. Answer the phone. I'm out. Come see me. 8343 S. Wolcott.*

Instantly, I got heated!

Dre? Baby? Who the fuck is this nigga?

"The fuck?" I muttered.

The text hadn't been opened, but she could have read that shit in the notifications on the top of the screen. Although Kennedy and I had only been together for two years before she went to prison, for five years we had been spiritually and emotionally connected. Our bond was tighter than a couple that had been married for thirty years, and I thought our loyalty was stronger than this. But shit, I had been hiding something from her, and I guessed she had been doing the same.

Talk about a nigga being pissed? I was heated! I couldn't get to that address fast enough! A nigga was steaming as I bent corners and blocks at damn near a hundred miles an hour. Once I arrived at the address and pulled in front of the small, single family home, I reached into the glove compartment and got my burner.

Whoever this nigga was, he was about to get *kilt*, and then I was going to drag Kennedy's ass out of there with Kayla on my hip.

I climbed out of the car, slammed the door shut, and raced toward the house. I banged on the door with the butt of my gun and even attempted to kick that motherfucker down!

Within seconds, some lil' nigga with green-ass eyes swung the door open, trying to look all threatening and shit, but was met with a gun in his face, so quickly he bitched up.

"Aye, man! What the fuck?!" he shouted with his hands up.

I forced my way inside, not even closing the door behind me. "Where the fuck is she?"

"Who?" He stared at me, wondering who the fuck was I was talking about.

My eyes burned into his as my nose flared. I grabbed his little ass around the neck while I pointed the gun straight at his temple. "Don't fucking play with me!"

Then it was like something dawned on him. As he stared at me, it was like something hit him and he realized something. "King?" he asked.

"Yeah, nigga, King! Now where the fuck is Kennedy?"

He had the nerve to fucking chuckle like shit was sweet and there wasn't a gun to his head. So I squeezed his neck tighter, and he threw his hands further into the air in surrender. "Aye! Aye! Cool out. It ain't like that. I'm Dre...*Drea*...her cellmate from the pen, man."

Drea. Kennedy had told me about her and Ms. Jerry so many times.

I let her neck go and put the gun down.

"She didn't know I was getting out this morning. I wanted to surprise her, but she hasn't hit me back." She noticed my frustration and asked, "You don't know where she's at?"

"Nah. I'm looking for her. She left her phone. I thought she might be here. Mind if I look around?"

She chuckled asking, "You don't believe me?"

I just gave her a cold, emotionless stare, giving her my answer.

So she nodded and said, "Go ahead. But this is my mama's house, so respect her shit."

She stayed in the living room while I looked through the small, two bedroom home. There was no sign of Kennedy or Kayla anywhere.

When I walked back into the living room, Dre was sitting comfortably on the couch. She seemed to notice that my demeanor had changed. I had gone from deadly to somber. This had been my last hope. Now I just felt hopeless.

"What's wrong? She's missing or something?" Dre asked.

"Kinda. She's mad at me, so hasn't come home yet." Then I just walked by Dre and went straight for the door. "If you talk to Ms. Jerry, ask her if she's talked to Kennedy."

I heard Dre sigh heavily. "I'm not gon' talk to Ms. Jerry. She's dead. She died Wednesday night."

Fuck. My steps halted slightly and I shook my head. *Something else that's going to break her heart.*

As I walked out of the door, I heard Dre say, "Please tell her to call me when you find her."

I just kept walking toward my ride. My feet were barely able to move because my body was so weighed down with guilt. I couldn't believe that I was putting Kennedy through this and I couldn't hold her to make it better. For three years, I hadn't been able to hold her to make it feel better, and now I was right back in the same situation because of some shit I had done. As I rode to the crib, I was literally sick, but I anticipated an angry Kennedy being there.

As I pulled into the garage, regret filled my heart when I realized that her car was nowhere to be found. I walked into a pitch black house, and my heart sank. She wasn't there, and by the looks off it, she hadn't been there.

I collapsed on the couch, feeling lost and helpless. I had forgotten about everything else, including Elijah and Siren. All I wanted was Kennedy. I had spent years feeling an unbearable yearning for that woman, and here that unbearable feeling was again. I hated it. I just wanted her to come back so that the feeling would go away.

I lay there until the sun came up, and my body began to heave as I realized that I had possibly lost Kennedy forever.

"Urrrgh!" I was sick to my fucking stomach as I began to dry heave. "Fuck!"

I rolled off of the couch and onto my knees. My head slowly fell to the carpet as my fingers clutched the fibers of it in anguish. I was a hurting man. I had spent three years missing Kennedy, and I had never wanted to feel that heartbreak again. Yet I was, just three weeks later. My body was rejecting that fucked up feeling, attempting to force it out through my throat.

Tears filled my eyes as they squeezed tightly together and my mind screamed, *Where the fuck is she?*

To be continued....

In order to receive a text message when *A Thug's Love 3* is released, send the keyword "Jessica" to 25827! Please leave me a review and check out some of my other work:

JESSICA'S CONTACT INFO:

Email: jessica.n_watkins@yahoo.com

Amazon page: http://ow.ly/LYLEL

Facebook: http://www.facebook.com/authorjwatkins

Facebook group:
http://www.facebook.com/groups/femistryfans

Twitter: @authorjwatkins

Instagram: @authorjwatkins

CPSIA information can be obtained
at www.ICGtesting.com
Printed in the USA
LVHW080830060219
606564LV00030B/428/P